SHEPHERDED TO DEATH

C.B. WILSON

eBook ISBN: 978-1-7374393-5-6

Print ISBN: 978-1-7374393-7-0

This is a work of fiction. Names, characters, institutions, events or locales in this novel are the product of the authors imagination or used fictitiously.

DEDICATION

For my amazing niece Sandy.
You inspire me everyday.

CONTENTS

1. Bow Wow Boutique
2. Posh Puppies
3. Bichon Bisquet
4. Beg-als Shoppe
5. Muttropolis
6. Woofing Best Coffe
7. Urban Pup
8. Snooty Pooch
9. Fluff & Buff
10. Fiesta Chihuahua
11. Bank
12. Gem's Palace
13. Blooming Tails
14. Taj Ma Hound
15. Hot Dog Stand
16. Bone Garden Salad
17. Attorney
18. Escrow
19. Hair Salon
DOG PATH
Cat's Town House
Homes
K9 Fine Wine Bar
Graveyard & Ghost
Hounds Hardware
Frosty Pup
Chateau Chienn
Salty Dog Seafood
Doodle Pad
Mutt Hutt
KDOG Studio
Farmer's Market
Dolce
Ciao Bella
Dog House
1st
2nd
3rd
4th
A Lifeguard Tower
B Old Barkview Inn
WOOF

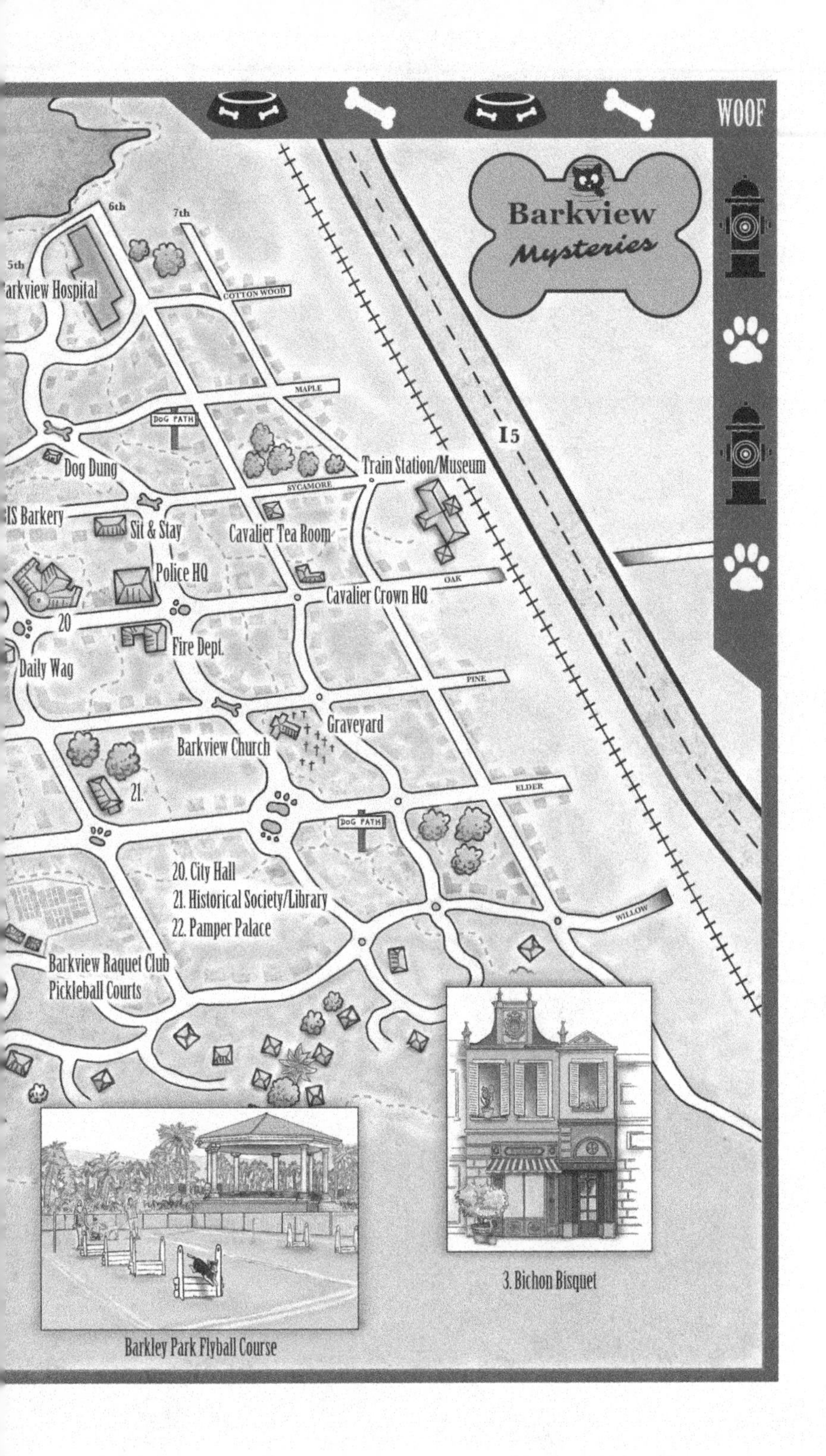

3. Bichon Bisquet
Barkley Park Flyball Course

CHARACTERS HUMAN

Barklay, Celeste: Founder of Barkview in 1890.

Barklay, Charlotte (Aunt Char): Mayor Barkview, Dog Psychiatrist on *Throw Him a Bone.* Renny, a champion King Charles Spaniel is her dog.

Barklay, JB: Aunt Char's late husband.

Bright, Alicia: Owns the Bow Wow Boutique. Misha, the Fashionista Yorkie, is her dog.

Douglas, Jonathon and Marie: Rum runner lost in 1925. Owner of the Douglas Diamond.

Duncan, Franklin: Old Barkview Inn concierge.

Hawl, Russ: Cat's boyfriend. FBI consultant. Owns Blue Diamond Security.

Le Fleur, Michelle: Owns Fluff and Buff Salon. Fifi, a black standard Poodle, is her dog.

Manyard, Ty: Aunt Char's assistant at City Hall.

Martinez-Vega, Angela: Director of security for the Gemology Institute of America (GIA).

McCarthy, Stephanie: Owns the Frosty Pup Creamery. BB, a Blue Bay Shepherd, is her dog.

Oldeman, Will: Old Barkview Inn elevator operator.

Madame Orr: Barkview's fortune teller/psychic. Danior, a Bellington Terrier, is her dog.

Papas, Ariana and Chris: Owners of Gem's Palace Jewelry. Gem, a German Shepherd, is their dog.

Princess Sophia: Princess of Dalsia.

Roma, Logan and Loreli: Brother and sister pickleball players. Contessa is Loreli's Cavalier King Charles Spaniel.

Roma, Victor Jr.: Owner of Firebird Industries.

Samuels, Isaac and Jacob: Brothers and owners of Samuels and Sons Jewelry Store.

Samuels, Ruby: Former wife of Jacob Samuels. A minority owner in Samuels and Sons Jewelry Store.

Schmidt, Gregory (Uncle G): Barkview's police chief. Max and Maxine, silver-point German Shepherds, are his dogs.

Smythe, Adam: Former Mayor of Barkview.

Smythe, Chelsea: Former Mayor's daughter.

Smythe, Linda: Deceased. Former Mayor's wife. Lady Mag, a Cavalier King Charles Spaniel, was her dog.

Tuner, Gabby: Owner of the Daily Wag Coffee Shop. Sal, a Saluki, is her dog.

Williams, Chad: Fortune hunter searching for the Douglas Diamond.

Wright, Catalina "Cat": Producer/investigative reporter at KDOG. A cat person living in Barkview.

Wynne, Sandy: Cat's assistant and computer wiz. Jack, a Jack Russell Terrier, is her dog.

CHARACTERS CANINE

🐾BB: Stephanie's Blue Bay Shepherd.

🐾Contessa (Tessa): Loreli's Tricolor Cavalier King Charles Spaniel.

🐾Danior: Madame Orr's Bellington Terrier.

🐾Fifi: Michelle Le Fleur's black standard Poodle.

🐾Gem: Ariana and Chris's tan-and-black female German Shepherd.

🐾Jack: Sandy's Jack Russell Terrier.

🐾Lady Mag: Lynda Smythe's Cavalier King Charles Spaniel.

🐾Max and Maxine: Uncle G's German Shepherds.

🐾Renny: Aunt Char's champion Cavalier King Charles Spaniel.

🐾Sal: Gabby's Saluki dog.

CHAPTER 1

Bad luck just kept coming. In fact, I swear a jinx hung over my aunt's first major mayoral event. Naturally, it had to be Barkview's high-profile Double Jubilee Founder's Day celebration. Who could've predicted a water main break flooding out the first two days of our Fetch-a-thon Pickleball Tournament or a winter storm dumping torrential downpours for three solid days? In addition to downed trees, sliding mud, and flooding, intermittent power outages threatened the security of our gala's centerpiece, an up-close showing of the 18.3-carat fancy yellow Shepard Diamond, on loan from the Smithsonian.

The moment the Daily Wag Coffee Bar's grandfather clock chimed 7 a.m., I glared at Sandy Wynne, my ever-perky blonde assistant and voice of Millennials, who had arranged this meeting. No charity-planning committee needed to convene before the sun even peeked through the clouds.

My name is Catalina Wright, Cat to my friends. I admit to not being a morning person. In fact, after years of working as an investigative reporter and producing KDOG's hit swing-shift cable show, *Throw Him a Bone*, only serious bribery got me out of bed before nine. Ariana Papas's tardiness really got to me. She resided above her store, Gem's Palace, only a short block away.

Coffee shop owner Gabby Turner pulled her cell phone from its holster on her black apron. Although her lanky, angular look brought a strung-out caffeine junkie to mind, Gabby's warm brown eyes and I'm-your-best-friend smile made everyone feel at home. With her anorexic lookalike Saluki plastered to her calf, Gabby shaped public opinion in her English garden–inspired courtyard one java at a time. "Ariana is never late. She walks Gem at six."

Getting up before dawn to walk a dog? Another reason I preferred independent, litter box–trained cats, a true four-letter word in Barkview, the self-proclaimed dog-friendliest city in America.

We all watched Gabby dial. When her call went directly to voicemail, my lingering sleep fog vanished. Something wasn't right. I could feel it.

"There must be a reasonable explanation." Gabby's hand shook as she reached across the English oak counter to top up my travel mug with her proprietary double-double caramel cappuccino. "You know Chris is out of town again."

That Ariana's husband seemed to be gone more than at home lately struck me as odd for a homebody goldsmith. No reason to panic yet. When you lived in Mayberry, a simple calendar snafu generally explained tardiness. Nothing ever happened in this quaint small town.

"I'll go check on her." Although Ariana was in fantastic shape for a woman pushing sixty-something, the steady rain patter made conditions hazardous. Best I make sure.

Gabby handed me my steaming cup with about-time finality. "Please let me know Ariana and Gem are okay."

I nodded. I let myself believe real concern drove that

request as I trotted past the antique oak tables and spindle chairs and onto the porch on the corner of Second and Maple Streets.

Sandy met me at my Jag SUV. After eighteen months working together, she anticipated my every move far too well. No way I'd freeze my knees off walking. In hopes of the sun breaking through the cloud cover and resuming tournament pickleball play, we'd both dressed in matching royal-blue tops and tennis-style skirts despite the very unseasonal Southern California weather. While Sandy's forever legs drew every eye in the A-line skort, I just got the *You're-insane* looks. Good thing I'd accepted my tawny girl-next-door looks years ago and didn't even try to compete.

"On the bright side, the drought is over." Sandy shook water droplets off her long, blonde mane.

"No kidding. Another inch and the hound playgrounds will need to be renamed pooch pools." Sandy's eye roll dissed my joke. What did she expect? I hadn't even finished my first coffee yet.

It took me less time to drive the six hundred feet to Gem's Palace on Fourth Street than to parallel park in front of the emerald-trimmed Victorian home. Framed by endless magenta bougainvillea, the porch invited shoppers to peek inside the big bay windows displaying dog-inspired gold and silver creations.

One look at the crooked CLOSED sign dominating the beveled glass door and that crazy twitter in my gut took hold —the same feeling I'd learned to trust when the Cavaliers had been dognapped and Howard Looc murdered. Sandy wasn't going to like this one bit.

"I have a feeling," I said.

Sandy paled. "What do you need me to do?" No hesitation. I liked that about her.

"Call Uncle G." I reached into my glove box and removed a heavy, black, weapon-quality flashlight before climbing out of the vehicle. Uncle G wasn't really a blood relative, but he was my Aunt Char's second husband's brother-in-law. Addressing him as "Uncle" saved me from making that convoluted explanation.

"Am I calling him as the chief of police or your uncle?" Two-carat sapphires stared back at me. No one interrupted the chief's breakfast without verifiable cause.

I took a deep breath. I really wanted to believe Ariana had overslept, but ... "Ariana's in trouble." I brandished the flashlight like the break-down-the-door club it was. Taking cover and waiting for the police to arrive was appealing, but something told me I couldn't wait. No way Ariana's overprotective German Shepherd had allowed anyone inside the shop. She had to be injured.

The doorknob turned easily and sent me right into hyperventilating mode. An unlocked jewelry store? Not on Ariana's watch. I threw open the door. The bomb-went-off disaster sucked the breath right out of me. Where once seven octagonal glass counters housed precious metal creations, only shattered glass mounds mixed with flashes of gold, silver, and precious stones remained. Even the crystal chandeliers had been pulled from the ceiling and lay in a heap of broken glass on the wood floor.

A smash-and-grab robbery in Barkview? But what had been grabbed? The bulk of the jewelry appeared to still be there, including my aunt's diamond Cavalier collection. I recognized several pieces she'd loaned to Ariana for a special showing scattered on the floor. Even the butter-soft tan leather barrel chairs had been overturned and slashed. Someone had been looking for something—something more valuable than Gem Palace's high-end merchandise and the diamond Cavalier collection. No sign of Ariana or Gem either.

A thousand possibilities came to mind. None of them good. "Ariana, are you here?"

A moan, so faint I barely heard it over the pounding in my ears, came from the backroom workshop—the same room that housed the store's vault for loose stones. Glass crunched beneath my athletic shoes like a thousand beetles, scattering every which way as I darted across the retail store. That I was disturbing a crime scene didn't even matter. Ariana was hurt, badly from the sound of it.

Flashlight ready, I flew through the door. I tripped over a black-and-tan fur mound that had to be Gem and sprawled forward, landing on my left shoulder on the tile floor with a thud. Ouch! I was going to feel that for sure.

I was still in better shape than Gem. She lay there unmoving but breathing, I realized with relief when I saw a dart sticking out of her neck bobbing with every breath. Tranquilizer darts? Not standard smash-and-dash burglar equipment. Someone had done their homework.

Another moan sent me scrambling to my feet. OMG! I'd fallen into a B-movie abduction scene. Dead center in the workroom lined with jewelers' tools sat a small hooded figure, zip-tied to a straight-backed chair.

I crossed the floor in three strides and ripped the pillowcase off Ariana's head. Gone was the not-a-hair-out-of-place woman I knew. Instead, unseeing eyes, framed by a white-blonde Einstein hairdo that would make any horror film junkie grin, greeted me. Her words—a chant, really, of "*Ich weiß nicht*" —bothered me most.

I recognized shock when I saw it. Why else would Ariana revert to her native language? I tapped her shoulder. "Ariana, it's Cat. I'm here to help."

She started. A sob ripped through her, the scary kind: half relief and half panic. "*Ich weiß nicht*," she muttered again.

"I don't understand." But I did. I didn't need to be fluent in German to understand that the villains hadn't found whatever they had been looking for.

Distant sirens shattered the silence. Help was almost here. I cut the zip-ties with a pair of scissors I found on the work-bench. Ariana rubbed her raw wrists. How long had she been bound?

I caught her as she stumbled to her feet. She felt like a china doll, fragile and unfocused. "*Juwel! Sie haben sie erschossen.*"

"I don't understand." I really didn't this time.

It took a second, but Ariana translated. "They shot Gem."

"With a tranquilizer dart," I said, pointing to the sleeping dog. All said, she was in better shape than Ariana.

"She bit the tall one on the arm." Anger replaced her blank-ness as she pointed to her right arm.

"How many were there?" Keeping her talking seemed to help.

"Two. A tall, skinny one and a shorter one."

"Men?"

More uncertainty. "I think so. They wore masks. The short one didn't talk."

"What did they want?" I asked.

"A diamond."

It had been a robbery. "What diamond? My aunt's Cavalier collection appears to still be here."

Ariana's fiery blue gaze locked with mine. "You must protect Gem."

Was it always about the dog? "Gem will be okay after the drugs wear off." If a head shake meant stirring, the dog was on her way back.

"Promise me you won't let her out of your sight." Ariana's intensity had to be situation-related. Gem never left her side.

"Me? She's a sixty-pound attack dog."

"They'll come back for her. She's the only one who can identify the killers."

"Killers?" I squeaked. "No one's dead."

"Chris is." Uncle G's familiar baritone stopped me cold. I gritted my teeth. Flanked by his pair of iron-gray German Shepherds that matched his neatly clipped beard and full head of hair, the chief of police proved my theory that masters choose physically similar canine companions.

Ariana's husband was dead. I expected her to faint, not stiffen and pull away, dry-eyed and determined.

"But you knew that," Uncle G continued, looking at Ariana. "We found him in the Crown Ballroom."

"With a fake Shepard Diamond." She collapsed against the wall, her back sliding downward until she was sitting on the tile floor.

I gasped. I couldn't help myself. "The Shepard Diamond's been stolen?"

"So it seems." Uncle G's nod confirmed everything.

Furballs! A priceless missing diamond, a murdered diamond cutter, and a jewelry store robbery in Barkview?

I'd never have suspected Ariana knew anything until her hand closed over my arm. "Promise me you will protect Gem."

Me, protect a German Shepherd? I glanced at the fur rug still blocking the door. No way! "Ariana ..."

"Promise me." Her hand grasped my forearm in a bruising iron grip. Who was this petite woman? Nothing made sense. No help came from Uncle G either. He just stood in the doorway with his arms crossed.

She couldn't be serious. "Why me?"

Ariana's finger brushed my cheek. "You will do what needs

to be done regardless of the consequences. I admire that in you. Don't let your aunt change you."

A compliment or a warning? I wasn't sure.

Ariana suddenly released me and stood stoically. "Entering the Witness Security Program isn't a guarantee of safety."

"Not when you go back to old associates," Uncle G said, unfazed. He'd known all along, from the looks of it.

It was my turn to lean against the wall for support. Witness protection was for people who testified against criminals. How was that even possible? Ariana and Chris were thirty-five-year Barkview residents. They supported local charities, donated to dog rescues, and spent Sundays holding hands in the park. They'd even created Aphrodite's Haven, a shiny, chain-link porch swing framed by potted blush roses on their porch, the go-to marriage proposal spot in town revered by a generation of Barkviewian romantics. Who were Ariana and Christos, really? And what secrets did they have?

CHAPTER 2

"Ariana must be devastated, losing Chris." Naturally, Aunt Char would be more concerned about Ariana's emotional well-being than the serious political and legal fallout she faced. Dressed in a classic Dior suit and seated behind her desk at City Hall, Aunt Char looked more like a reigning Nordic monarch than a beach city mayor. Renny, her champion Cavalier King Charles Spaniel, sat sphinx-style on a chair beside her. Behind her a picture window framed by cut-glass side windows overlooked the Oak Street gas lamps. Constructed from local sandstone brick with a pitched roof and elegant redwood accents, City Hall epitomized the unique elegance we all called Barkview. Inside, the office reflected the likes and dislikes of its many predecessors. No doubt the crystal vase of cheery sunflowers would be my aunt's addition.

"Oddly, she seemed resigned. It's almost like she'd been prepared for years for this to happen." I laid out a line of Post-it notes, my go-to note-taking tool despite Sandy's computers-rule influence. Some things just needed to be written down. What Ariana had to say certainly qualified. She'd told me as much as she could in the fifteen minutes or so before the US Marshal arrived to place her in protective custody.

"Perhaps the shock hasn't worn off yet," Aunt Char suggested.

"Maybe. Ariana and Chris were gymnasts who defected from East Germany during the 1972 Olympics." I paced the length of my aunt's book-lined office. "Did you know?" I asked.

Aunt Char steepled her hands. "No. I did suspect she and Chris were more than they let on, but everyone has secrets, my dear."

No kidding. This one topped the secret scale, for sure. "Ariana told me one hundred seventeen athletes defected from communist bloc countries in 1972."

"Eleven Israelis were killed in the Palestinian hostage situation as well," Aunt Char reminded me.

"How do you remember that? You were, like, ten." I barely remembered my senior prom. Of course, my many dating disasters tended to fall into the wipe-from-memory category.

"Reading history isn't the same as living it," Aunt Char explained.

No argument from me. "Ariana and Chris escaped together. Ariana was only sixteen. Who even thinks about finding their soulmate at that age?" I'd still been wearing braces.

"Sometimes you just know the right one," Aunt Char said.

Handsome and sexy Russ Hawl came to mind. Next week we'd celebrate our seven-month dating anniversary. Could I make a forever commitment even today?

Aunt Char's raised brow questioned more than I cared to think about. I changed the subject. "Chris made a deal to get them out of Germany."

"A deal with the devil, it appears."

"Apparently, Craigslist for defectors wasn't around back then, and you took what you could get. A high-end art-theft gang needed a gymnast for a job, and they snuck him and Ariana out of Germany."

"He traded one master for another," Aunt Char said. "So that's how Chris became a jewel thief."

"Ariana said it started with museum art thefts and graduated to jewelry, where he found his calling. He ultimately testified against the gang, and he and Ariana went into the Witness Security Program."

"All these years later, how did the thieves find him?"

"That's the question. Chris and Ariana changed their names and their physical appearance when they entered the protection program. A month ago Chris received a call to meet someone at the Barkview train station museum."

Aunt Char exhaled. "There are no cameras there."

Or anywhere else in Barkview. The price of quaintness continued to climb. Would there be a call to update the policy? Would Aunt Char champion the change? Traffic cameras alone would provide evidence for all sorts of crimes. "Ariana swears they didn't reach out to anyone. It could have been as simple as the thieves coming to Barkview to scope out the Shepard Diamond's security and recognizing him."

"Quite a coincidence."

Call me a skeptic, but I agreed. Chris looked nothing like the forty-year-old, faded black-and-white photo Ariana had showed me. "Ariana is in protective custody."

"Where's the Shepard Diamond now?" Aunt Char asked.

That was the question. "Ariana claims not to know."

"You don't believe her?"

I squirmed under Aunt Char's scrutiny. It wasn't that I didn't believe Ariana, exactly. This crazy feeling she knew much more ate at me. "I don't know what to believe," I finally said. "Ariana has been lying to us forever."

"With good reason." Why my aunt seemed okay with all

this made me wonder what other secrets were hidden in this dog-crazy town.

"The thieves blew the safe, not to mention ripped the store apart. Ariana's look around seemed cursory," I said.

"The Shepard Diamond is only about the size of a juicy summer grape."

"True. Ariana seemed more interested in introducing me to Gem's pack than looking for the diamond."

"She is your ward now," Aunt Char said.

"Don't remind me." I collapsed into the straight-backed desk chair. I'd agreed to watch the dog until Ariana got her new plan from the witness protection folks. That little ceremony Ariana had performed, adding me to Gem's pack, hadn't been a lifelong commitment. Or had it?

On cue, Gem entered with Sandy in tow. She dropped a pink duffle bag at my feet and promptly handed me the dog's leash. "What's in the bag? Rocks?" I asked.

"A bowl, some toys, and other stuff."

I didn't ask. The size and sound indicated a lot of stuff.

"I'll put her dog food right in your car."

That couldn't be good. Sandy hauled a twenty-pound camera around just to be prepared.

"Vet says she'll be a little sluggish for a day or so, but she'll have no long-term issues," Sandy informed me.

I shuddered. I couldn't help myself. What exactly had I agreed to? Gem's stone-studded leash attached to a matching collar felt like a dead weight. Me, responsible for a twenty-five-inch-tall attack dog with a tail that cleared coffee tables? A growling TV canine was enough to cause a channel change in my house.

Gem sat at attention at my feet, her presence seemingly walling me in behind her. No. My imagination had to be working overtime. The dog just sat next to me, her head cocked to the right while she watched everything.

"Good heavens, Cat, pet Gem. She's as confused as we all are," Aunt Char urged. "She's been trained with the same commands we use with the Barklay Cavaliers."

Good news in this mess. At least I was familiar with how to communicate with the dog. I still gulped. "Ariana warned me that Gem has stomach issues that sound a lot like doggie IBS." Who knew that was even possible?

Aunt Char's wide-eyed surprise made me question my conclusion. "I never knew that. Come to think of it, I've never seen Gem eat."

"Good thing you have experience dealing with Bayle's pancreatitis," Sandy said.

More like I'd lived in a constant state of panic when I dog-sat for my sorority sister's Bichon Frise. How did I end up with another dog with health issues?

"At least IBS isn't deadly. The vet said you just need to watch what she eats and make sure she poops at least once a day," Sandy explained.

Me, worrying about a dog's potty practices? This had to be some cosmic joke. Controlling the muscle-bound hairball seemed more daunting. First rule with dogs: show no fear. Yeah, right. Visions of growling Pit Bulls from my past knocking me to my knees weren't going away.

Renny saved me. With Queen Cavalier poise, she stretched, leaped to the ground, and circled Gem, finally sitting eye to eye with the larger dog. A snack in the German Shepherd eating order, Renny still didn't give an inch until Gem shook her head and crouched.

"What just happened?" I asked, but I knew. Renny had just put Gem on notice. Not a sound had been uttered, but the larger dog knew who was boss. Admirable, really.

Renny acknowledged my thanks with a head toss and a don't-mess-this-up look.

No doubt I'd need a repeat performance in no time. I scratched Gem's head. The faster I found Chris's murderer and the Shepard Diamond, the faster I could return her. If Ariana was right and the dog could recognize the killers, all I had to do was let Gem lead me to them. The problem was that pickleball tournament enthusiasts had been traipsing through Gem's Palace all week. Could Gem find the scent of the murderers among all the tourists? Better yet, could I interpret what Gem tried to tell me? I didn't speak dog.

Enough lamenting. Aunt Char had bigger problems than me coping with a well-trained dog.

"So, the big question here is, how do you want to handle the press on the missing diamond, Madam Mayor?" I asked more formally.

"I hardly think there's a choice, my dear."

"But there is. Uncle G found Chris clutching a near-perfect Shepard Diamond replica."

Aunt Char smiled. A good surprise for a change. "How did he know the diamond wasn't real?"

"He didn't at first. Ariana told him. Testing confirmed the stone is lab created. The interesting part is that the replica has the correct laser-etched ID number."

"How is that possible?" Aunt Char asked.

"Apparently that was Chris's specialty. He replaced stolen gems with near-perfect fakes. Ariana said Chris had locked himself in his workroom for the past two weeks. She found yellow-diamond residue on his laser cutter. That means Chris had the exact specifications long before the diamond arrived in Barkview."

More good news. "So, it's a Smithsonian or Gemological Institute of America problem," Sandy suggested.

"We can blame anyone we want, but the fact remains the gem was stolen in Barkview."

"It is a Barkview problem," Aunt Char announced with finality.

"It's actually a frightening thought since both institutions house priceless, irreplaceable stones," I said. "Does makes you wonder how many exhibitions show duplicated stones."

"It is unreal the Smithsonian could have delivered a fake diamond," Sandy said.

"Ariana doesn't think they did. Chris always ordered two roughs to create the replicas in case the first cutting wasn't exact. We couldn't find a second rough, and the villains questioning Ariana kept saying, 'He's not doing it again.' Apparently, Chris switched a fake diamond for the real one on his last job with the gang."

"Quite ingenious," Aunt Char said.

"If you don't get caught." In the end, Chris had paid the ultimate price.

"I still can't believe Chris was murdered in the Old Barkview Inn's historic Crown Ballroom," Aunt Char said.

"Yes. Shot with a poison dart and left with the fake diamond in his hand beside the ballroom display case," I explained. "The chief has requested a rush on the autopsy to isolate the poison."

Sandy whistled. "So, it was a double double-cross."

She had a point. No honor among thieves here.

"How did Chris get by the top-of-the-line ballroom security? The chief assured me the heat sensors and laser-grid surveillance would catch a mosquito." My aunt's practical side always came out.

I shrugged. "I don't know exactly how the technology failed." Since Uncle G had hired Blue Diamond Security to design the system, as the owner, Russ faced scrutiny as well.

"Apparently, Chris was not your average jewel thief," I continued. "In fact, the FBI dubbed him the Phantom M after a World War II spy/British magician named Jasper Maskelyne. Chris supposedly never revealed his methods, but somehow got in and out of impossible places during his heists. Ariana told me Chris's mother made a good living as a circus contortionist."

Aunt Char grinned. "She taught her son her secrets well."

Depending on your definition of "well." Although Chris Papas had hidden his abilities behind a professorial persona, complete with horn-rimmed glasses, he'd still been murdered. It was still hard to believe he could squeeze through the ballroom's turret windows and scale the slick walls without Spiderman skills.

"Because we have a stone, do you think the diamond exhibition can continue?" Aunt Char asked.

"Yes. Both the Smithsonian and the GIA have ample reason to keep the incident quiet while we investigate."

Aunt Char exhaled. "Whoever has the diamond will get away with the crime. That is not acceptable."

"Only Ariana, the chief, you, me, Sandy, and Russ know the truth. If Chris followed his usual MO, then he replaced the real stone before it came to Barkview. That's what Ariana believes. We're confident the thieves don't have it either since they went after Ariana."

"You think he broke into the Gemological Institute of America? The security in that place is worse than Area 51." Talk about awe. It took a lot to impress Sandy.

Repeated, the thought sounded even more preposterous than when Ariana had voiced it. Chris breaking into the GIA? The priceless gems were under intense 24/7 scrutiny. How could he have done it?

Aunt Char paced the length of her desk, processing everything. Finally, she said, “I will agree to the GIA and FBI’s best strategy to catch Chris’s killer and retrieve the diamond. The culprit must be caught.”

Leave it to Aunt Char to be more concerned with doing what was right than protecting her own political career. Assuming there was a real diamond somewhere to be found, finding this stone wasn’t going to be easy. If Ariana didn’t know where Chris hid it, how was I supposed to find it? Sandy and I had been looking for Barkview’s very own treasure, the lost Douglas Diamond, for almost two years now with no luck. Some might say I’m diamond-challenged. The only way I’d figure this out was to go back to basics. Chris’s past hadn’t just found him after all these years. Something or someone had brought it all together.

“Do you know why Adam Smythe wanted the Shepard Diamond as part of the Double Jubilee celebration events?” The previous mayor’s relentless pursuit of the famous yellow diamond during the election campaign suddenly seemed suspicious.

“He said he wanted a big gesture to mark our one-hundred-and-twenty-year anniversary,” Aunt Char replied.

“Why that stone? It has no historic significance to Barkview or anyplace else. It was named after the Smithsonian employee who acquired it.” I knew my diamond history. ”The stone was traded for loose diamonds the US Customs Service had confiscated back in 1958. It’s an odd trade for a significant yellow diamond.”

“Could he have learned the diamond’s history?” Sandy asked. “The former mayor is a history buff with time on his hands.”

“Too much time, if you ask me. The Shepard Diamond’s past seems to be a go-to-the-grave secret. No records existed. Unless Adam found a random reference in a private diary...” I said. "He's been a problem since you took office. It would be just like him to steal the spotlight with a revelation."

"Don't be so hard on the man, my dear. He did lose his wife and his job last year."

All might be fair in love and politics, but only Aunt Char could forgive the man's ugly smear campaign. I needed to apply a little of her understanding when I spoke with him.

"I'll chat with Ty. One assistant to another." Sandy winked at me.

"Good plan." Aunt Char had retained her predecessor's assistant, Ty Maynard, despite loyalty concerns—a testament to her kind heart. "Adam didn't do all the research himself."

Sandy scratched Gem's head. "Take care of her."

I wasn't sure if she was talking to Gem or me. "Are you sure you can't..."

"Jack's already incorrigible. Not a chance Gem would make it in my house."

From the perspective of sheer size, the German Shepherd should prevail, but Sandy's Jack Russell Terrier did define perpetual motion. He drove everyone crazy.

"Ariana trusted you with Gem," Aunt Char pointed out.

No help coming from her. In all fairness, twelve Cavalier King Charles Spaniels currently resided in the Barklay Kennel, eight of which were puppies in training. "Russ is going to sneeze his head off." Only I could have a boyfriend allergic to dogs.

I couldn't miss Aunt Char's knowing grin. "Are the allergy shots working?"

"Too early to tell." I still couldn't believe he'd suggested the desensitizing program. Two shots a week? Ugh.

Aunt Char handed me a fresh supply of Barkview's herbal allergy pills just in case. "He's doing it for you."

And one day he'd decide I wasn't worth it. He'd also kept

the lease on the beach house down the boardwalk from me despite accepting a new assignment with Blue Diamond Security in Los Angeles. "I don't know how this is going to work out." I hadn't meant to say it out loud, or had I? Ariana and Chris's love story had got me thinking too much.

"Why? You are both intelligent, independent people who care about each other," Aunt Char insisted. "JB and I started the same way."

"Hardly. You gave up everything for him." I'd been shocked when they'd married after a whirlwind romance.

"I left a TV announcer job, that did not fulfill me, to come to Barkview." Her wistful smile confirmed that JB had been the love of her life. Lost too soon.

No denying the similarities between Ariana and Chris's story and my aunt's. They'd both sacrificed their careers for a chance to be with the man they loved. Was I willing to do that for Russ?

Gem butted her head against my leg, nearly knocking me over as she leaned into my knee. I grabbed the chair back for balance. Enough lamenting. I had a job to do.

"I'm meeting Uncle G at the Old Barkview Inn. He's interviewing potential witnesses. Let's hope Gem recognizes someone." Ariana had insisted she would. How I'd know if the dog did remained a mystery. "I'll call you when I have new information."

CHAPTER 3

Gem walked on my left side about five inches from my leg, pausing and quick-stepping in sync with my pace all the way to my car. So, this was how the heel command worked. My aunt's Cavalier had best watch out. I knew the rules now.

With this kind of cooperation, I considered walking the six or so blocks to the Old Barkview Inn, but the steady drip-drop of rain made that decision easy. Time to give up on the pickleball skirt too. Even if the sun miraculously came out, the concrete tennis-style courts would never dry fast enough to resume play today.

I opened my Jag's passenger-side front door and motioned Gem inside. She paused, her black nose sniffing upward. I sniffed too, half afraid I'd locate a moldy lunch bowl. Nothing foul. I motioned the dog to enter again. No movement. Lifting a fifteen-pound Cavalier into the car hardly required Herculean strength, but a full-size German Shepherd? I tried one more time. With a head shake and a single fluid leap, Gem landed on the passenger seat, tan-and-black fur scattering like dandelion seeds.

I gritted my teeth as I closed the door. At least German Shepherd fur settled like easy-to-vacuum fluff on my seat, versus those Jack Russell needle hairs Sandy's dog left embedded in my carpet.

I climbed in on the driver's side. Gem sat at eye level with me. No question I met Barkview carpool rules. My windshield wipers flapped back and forth as I drove west on Oak Street. When I turned left on First Street, the sky-blue-and-white gingerbread trim on the Old Barkview Inn peeked through the fog.

The most photographed building in Barkview, the late-Victorian-era structure had hosted countless Hollywood productions featuring the majestic beachfront widow's walk connecting twin turrets. Today, three police SUVs blocked the valet entrance, promising me a wet walk from the parking lot.

Naturally, Gem leaped out of the car into a puddle, splattering my once-upon-a-time white court shoes with a sandy, muddy mess. Could this day get any worse?

I had to ask. A second later, the threatening clouds burst, and drowned-cat pretty much summed up our arrival in the hotel's elegant marble entry. Concierge Franklin Duncan, dressed in a Victorian waistcoat and gentleman's ascot, met us at the double doors. Any question he took customer service to a level five-star resorts could only aspire to disappeared the moment he handed me a warm, lavender-scented towel. I thanked him with a sigh.

"Nasty day out there, Miss Wright." Franklin knelt beside Gem, wrapping her in another towel.

"Outside and in." The police barricade outside the ballroom entry drew my eye away from the hand-carved mahogany ceiling molding and ocean-inspired, stained-glass windows.

"Indeed. Imagine, Mr. Papas killed protecting the Shepard Diamond. I don't know what to say."

Neither did I. Uncle G's tall tale pretty much said it all.

"The chief requested that you join him in the Windsor Suite." Franklin handed me a chiffon-tied toiletry pouch.

Self-consciously, I patted my damp, tawny ponytail. I had pulled my hair back to get an upper hand on a bad hair day. Had I failed that miserably?

Franklin's answer made perfect sense. "Mr. Hawl is in the ballroom."

Ah. Russ had arrived from Los Angeles in record time. I glanced at my limp shirt and mud-splattered shoes. So much for my aunt's preparedness training. At this point in our relationship, Russ knew model-perfect wasn't the real me.

I still appreciated Franklin's thoughtfulness and thanked him as I headed to the Centurion Otis 61 elevator. Originally powered by steam, the ornate wrought iron elevator had been converted to electric around the time of Ariana's defection in the early 1970s. Two events I'd now forever associate.

The gate slid open, and I greeted the ancient elevator operator. Dressed in starched dark tails and a Victorian striped waistcoat, Will Oldeman had the distinction of being the oldest continuous employee in the Old Barkview Inn and the most well-informed.

Nose first, Gem lunged inside, almost dislocating my shoulder in her haste. So much for heeling. Will shuffled into the dog's path, effectively ending further exploration. "Welcome, Miss Wright."

Gem generously permitted me to enter and then stepped in front of me, blocking the exit.

Will addressed Gem with a nod and then spoke. "The chief is expecting you both. The GIA's security director is with him."

"Angela Cooper requested an appointment with my aunt as well," I said.

Gem's pointed ears twitched and she sat at attention, alert for who knew what. "What is it with this dog?"

"She's protecting you, Miss Wright," Will explained.

"From what?"

"Any possible threat. It's the Shepherd's way."

Way to drive me insane. I'd been tasked with protecting her. No odds on the outcome of this power struggle. "Any guests Gem should meet?" I'd given up subtlety with Will years ago. The man knew everything anyway.

"Mr. Samuels has been in residence since last Thursday."

Why would Ariana's rival staff a small satellite hotel shop when his big-city storefronts reportedly brought in more revenue? "He did lobby for the Shepard Diamond's Barkview exhibition," I said. Truthfully, the whole alliance between Barkview's previous mayor and the uptown Samuels brothers bothered me.

Will's eye roll voiced his opinion without words.

"Where is Samuels staying?" I asked.

"The Hampton Court Suite." Will's expression remained unchanged, but I got his point. A junior suite with a garden view hardly fit the man's elevated opinion of himself.

The elevator slowed to a halt at the second floor. I swear Gem tapped her paw while waiting for Will to slide open the cage door.

"Who had the Windsor Suite before the chief appropriated it?" I asked.

"Miss Loreli and Mr. Logan."

"The pickleball brother-and-sister pro team from Arizona?"

"Very accommodating. Tessa, short for Contessa, Miss

Loreli's tricolor, is a Barklay Cavalier." Will's squared shoulders showed his pride in my aunt's champion kennel.

Aunt Char bred chestnut-colored Cavaliers. A white, tan, and black dog had to be a second- or third-generation mix, but was family in Will's eyes nonetheless. "I'll thank her for her support."

"She is staying for the gala. She feels like Barkview is her home," Will added.

No surprise. Dog people loved Barkview. Too bad the professional pickleball exhibition had been flooded out. Not by the rain, but by a broken water main. Hopefully the competition would be rescheduled. I wanted to see the brother-and-sister team play on the courts.

"Any thoughts on how the murderer got into the Crown Ballroom?" Russ, in cooperation with the GIA's security team, had set up the surveillance system. No doubt it was exceptional.

"Before the renovation, the Crown Ballroom's ceiling stood ten inches higher," Will announced.

That cavernous twenty-foot-high room had been even taller? "They put in a false ceiling?"

"Yes. The renovation team discovered that when they installed the new sprinkler system that the acoustics improved when the ceiling was lower. The sprinkler system required a four-inch drop. After some experimenting, they discovered that the additional ten inches made the sound resonate."

Certainly not something musically illiterate me would notice. Of course, what did I know about angles and sound waves? "Ten inches isn't enough space for even a small man to crawl through."

"Add that to the eight inches already there..."

"And you get entrée." We shared a knowing look. "Brilliant, Will. How would you access it?"

"The cupola fire escape." He continued before I could ask. "Some things a gentleman does not tell, Miss Wright."

I swallowed my grin. His flushed cheeks could only mean a romance. Curiosity gnawed at me, but I had learned that some secrets should not be told. "Who knows about this?"

"A good question," Will said. "The ceiling drop is listed as four inches on the original plans."

"The contractor and general manager had to have known." I scratched my head. "And the sound technician." Or whatever they were called in the 1970s. It would be easy enough to round up that group. The question was, how had Chris found out?

CHAPTER 4

A uniformed officer met Gem and me at the elevator and escorted us to the Windsor Suite. Named for Renny's great-great-great-great (however many greats it was) grandmother, fondly called the Queen Mum, the suite's sweeping views included Bark Rock and the coastal caves along the rugged coastline. Decorated in shades of apple green and cream, the clean lines and more modest curves of the mahogany settee and chairs popular during the late Victorian period invited conversation. Above the fireplace hung a portrait of the room's namesake who, I swear, stared right into a guilty soul.

The GIA's security director, Angela Cooper, clearly agreed, given the way she perched on the edge of the settee, her back ramrod-straight. Dressed in a chic pantsuit and heeled boots, her dark hair pulled back with a unique antique silver comb, she made me feel like something-the-cat-dragged-in frumpy. Of course, time under Uncle G's perceptive scrutiny and that of his two German Shepherd deputies could unnerve anyone unaccustomed to Barkview's dog-centric lifestyle.

Gem, the third German Shepherd in the room, made the

intimidation worse. She stopped in the entry and growled, a low, menacing sound that made my neck hairs take notice.

Angela jumped about a foot off the settee. Not that I blamed her. Shepherd bullying crackled around us. Was Gem trying to give me the murderer signal for Angela?

Apparently not. When Uncle G motioned Gem to stand down and the dog backed off with a mere toss of her elegant head, real frustration settled in. How was I supposed to differentiate between dog bravado, familiarity, and deadly recognition?

I moved toward the settee opposite Angela. Gem had another plan. No kidding. She herded me, nudging my leg every step I took toward the wing-back chair closest to the window. When I took the seat, Gem sat at attention beside me, guarding my flank. I'd be flattered if the whole incident didn't scream manipulation. By a dog? Now I was losing it. I controlled the dog. Theoretically, anyway.

I pulled out my ever-ready Post-its and snatched the Old Barkview Inn pen from the table beside the phone. Uncle G rolled his eyes and introduced me as the mayor's representative.

Angela's inky eyes, dwarfed by her wire-rimmed glasses, instantly softened. "The chief tells me the mayor is willing to keep this incident quiet while we investigate."

"She is." Angela's eagerness made me wonder if the woman had her own agenda.

"Good." Angela inspected her French manicure. "I spoke with the FBI major theft unit leader and he is in agreement as well. We must catch the culprit. Diamonds cannot go missing on my watch."

No kidding. The GIA graded priceless gems daily. Even a hint of impropriety associated with the integrity of security protocols could cause irrevocable damage.

As usual, Uncle G got right to the point. "Evidence suggests that the theft occurred while the diamond was under GIA control. Who had access to the Shepard Diamond?"

"A select group of longtime employees. Blue Diamond Security handled both the transfer from the Smithsonian to the GIA and from the GIA to the Old Barkview Inn." Angela's inference threw Russ right under the bus.

Arms crossed, Uncle G looked as unmovable as Gibraltar. "There is no indication of theft at transfer. Evidence points to an inside job."

Angela bristled. "No one penetrated our in-house security."

Her certainty made me wonder if Chris Papas could have breached GIA's security without leaving a trace. "You confirmed the diamond's authenticity on arrival from the Smithsonian?" Maybe the theft had occurred before the Shepard Diamond left the Smithsonian.

Angela's hesitation spoke volumes. "We, uh, checked the inscription on arrival."

"That's standard procedure?" There had to be more to taking possession of a priceless national treasure than a simple inscription check.

"Yes. The inscription is a confidential identification code assigned to the diamond on acquisition. We were scheduled to clean and regrade after the Barkview and GIA's Colored Diamond exhibition."

"When was the diamond last graded?" Uncle G asked.

Angela shuffled through her notes. "The Shepard Diamond was last cleaned and graded in 2012."

Ugh. I sank deeper into the soft cushions. In nine years, Chris could've been in and out of the Smithsonian numerous times. He had broken into the Louvre with no one the wiser.

"I'm investigating anyone who touched the diamond. So far, nothing suspicious," Angela insisted.

Of course not. Vetting people for money or family irregularities occurred prehire at the GIA. My reporter's mind defaulted to the bigger questions: why and why now? Only someone with something major to hide traded an eighteen-carat yellow diamond for nondescript miscellaneous smaller "currency" diamonds. The Smithsonian's Shepard Diamond story screamed conspiracy. "What is the diamond's real story?"

"I only know what the Smithsonian has published," Angela said.

That her dark gaze refused to meet mine said otherwise. "Let me ask this another way," I said. "The Smithsonian claims the diamond originated in South Africa. How can they know that? I thought isolating the region of origin or specific mine wasn't possible." My diamond studies were coming in handy today.

"That's true. I'm guessing the seller disclosed that information."

"This oh-so-honest seller?" I had to add.

Angela ignored my inference. "What was said or not said in 1958 may be irrelevant."

That little bombshell got both my and Uncle G's full attention.

Angela continued, "We have new technology we planned to test during the grading process that will isolate the atoms. We think we will be able to pinpoint when and where the stone was formed. Possibly when it was mined as well. The technology will not only identify once-lost stones, but offers a new way to end the sale of conflict diamonds."

I shared a glance with Uncle G. With the *Why now* question answered, *Why* still nagged at me. "So, potentially you can determine if the Shepard Diamond was, let's say, the lost Florentine Diamond?"

"No likely. The Florentine Diamond was greenish yellow in

color. The Shepard Diamond is a vivid fancy yellow," Angela explained.

"True, but whoever went to great lengths to protect the origin of the Shepard Diamond could be exposed."

Did Angela balk? She recovered so quickly I wasn't sure. "That was sixty years ago. Who could possibly care now?"

"Someone with a lot to lose or gain if the truth comes out." A public figure came to mind. Talk about an endless possibilities list.

"I will need the list of people who know about this technology," Uncle G told her.

"I've already investigated the group," Angela protested.

"This is a murder investigation. I will investigate them again." Uncle G didn't budge.

Angela just nodded. She recognized a no-win situation when she faced it.

Time to take Gem to the scene of the crime. I excused myself as Uncle G dove into the usual procedural questions. Another officer escorted me to the Crown Ballroom.

Before I could stop her, Gem bolted past the uniformed police guard and dragged me into the octagonal room, recognizable as a throne room in Hollywood films. The dark paneling framed both the larger bay and smaller transom windows, while conical chandeliers hung from the twenty-five-foot ceiling, completing a royal picture.

Today, glass display cases housing precious colored-diamond jewelry dominated the center of the room. No indication remained that someone had been murdered there hours earlier. In fact, the room looked serene and untouched.

Gem flopped down on the floor beside the elevated Shepard Diamond case and wailed a long, heartbroken Bassett-Hound howl that vibrated around me, echoing until I covered my ears. Talk about Sensurround! Will's acoustical assessment made perfect sense.

I heard Russ sneeze long before I spotted a rope drop from the ceiling and his descent with hand-over-hand precision. His normally conservative polo shirt emphasized his straining biceps and swimmer's build. I sucked in my breath. I did miss our daily beach walks from when he'd resided in Barkview. More than I wanted to admit.

Gem glanced at Russ and quietly took an attentive position at the rope's base. I half-expected trouble, but the dog ducked her head to encourage Russ to pet her. Whew. He passed. She liked him. Of course she did. What wasn't to like about a knight in shining armor anyway?

Still, I winced as fur floated every which way. He kissed my cheek as I handed him Celeste Barklay's allergy pills. The allergy shots weren't working. "Bloodshot" already described his blue eyes.

Russ downed the homeopathic pills dry. "Chris was set up."

No surprise there. "How did you find the rope?"

"Will pointed me in the right direction."

I smiled. Working on the Bichon case with me had given Russ some valuable insight into Barkview dynamics.

"The killer shot Chris with a lethal dart." He pointed to his neck, about where I'd find his carotid artery. "Autopsy will tell us what compound they used."

"The same dart that knocked out Gem?" I asked.

"Appears so." He scratched Gem's head. "But the compound had to be different. Chris died instantly. He fell..." He gestured from the ceiling to the floor.

"The killer had two different poison compounds? Isn't that strange?"

Russ nodded. "Leads me to believe they intended to kill Chris."

A shiver shinnied down my spine. "Maybe this is all about Chris's past." Why else kill a talented jewel thief?

Russ shook his head. "A dart gun as a murder weapon isn't organized-crime issue."

He should know. "How did you find the ceiling door?"

"I climbed the cupola fire escape and followed the acoustical maze to the rope. That maze was no easy task, I can assure you. Without these"—He held up twin palm-size suction cups—"I would not have made it through."

Nothing too special or unique about the equipment. "How...?"

"Found them cupped in Chris's palms."

Chris's trade secret revealed. "How did you navigate through the maze?"

"I followed the dust-free lanes. Question is, how did Chris know the way?"

Good question. At the very least, someone had provided the nonpublic plans. "How tight was the maze?"

"My nose scraped the flooring the entire way. I called in a forensic team to swab for DNA."

I bit back my smile. Russ's shoulder span dwarfed Chris's, which meant the murderer had also been small-statured or thin and definitely not claustrophobic.

"Exactly what Will said." I made a note to send the man a bag of my Woofing Best coffee stash. He'd earned it today. "Who filed the official plans?"

"Pacific Coast Construction. They had a branch in Barkview until 1998. The new owner, Firebird Industries, is headquartered in San Francisco."

Could it be that easy? I barely controlled a smirk. "The

former mayor, Adam Smythe—his family founded Pacific Coast Construction."

"That merits further investigation."

Say no more. My mission included proving Adam's public impropriety. "We know how Chris got to the Crown Ballroom. How did he get past your high-tech electronics?"

"Coordination and planning. When the water main break interrupted electrical service to the Old Barkview Inn, it shorted the heat sensors."

"I'm guessing I stand a better chance of winning the Mega Millions lottery than that scenario just happening."

Russ nodded. "Correct. The switch from grid to generator power also disabled the infrared sensors for three minutes and twenty seconds before the reset activated."

"Chris got in, got the diamond, and got out in three minutes?" Shinnying up and down the rope had to take most of the time.

"Like I said, a well-executed plan." Russ's jaw tightened. "Chris was a skilled jewel thief. I have no doubt he could execute his part. Sabotaging the water main took a special skill set."

"And a City of San Diego connection." Something Adam Smythe's government contacts could have arranged.

"The chief is investigating that angle." Russ scratched his head.

"Impressed?" I asked.

"I am. The timing was impeccable."

No small feat there. "Uncle G wants us to play our hand, so to speak. He hopes that continuing the exhibition will make the thieves believe we do not know the stone is a fake and so they will continue to search for it."

"Explain," Russ said.

"Since the thieves interrogated Ariana about the location of the real stone, we must assume they believe Chris swapped it with the fake for his own purposes."

"You know what they say about assuming," Russ stated.

Did I ever. We were banking on a lot of ifs. "GIA already discussed allowing the exhibition to go on with the FBI." I'd agree to any plan that helped Aunt Char weather the scandal. "Does this kind of thing happen often?"

"Often enough." He stopped my follow-up question with a head shake. "Don't ask. You know I can't talk about cases." His tone didn't give an inch.

I bit my lip. I knew the rules, but the secret nature of his job still drove me crazy. Instead I said, "I'd like to know how Adam Smythe and the Samuels brothers arranged to get the Shepard Diamond for the Barkview exhibit."

"They are an unlikely trio," Russ agreed. "I understand Isaac Samuels is in residence here."

"Wanna come talk to him with me?" We'd solved Howard Looc's murder together. With any luck, we could get Chris's killer too.

I followed Russ's gaze to the propped-open ceiling panel. "I'm tied up right now." He stroked my cheek with his forefinger. "My gut is telling me that this case isn't going to be black and white."

I swallowed hard. Russ's intuition tended to be right on. Why mine wasn't speaking to me bothered me no small amount. Maybe I wasn't close enough yet.

Russ continued, "Much as I'd prefer you stayed out of this until we better understand Chris's involvement, I know I can't stop you from asking questions. Be careful. Trust your instincts and Gem's."

That he hadn't told me to stay away said a lot. I relished his faith, reminding me partnerships went both ways. "Assuming the courts are dry enough to play pickleball tomorrow, will you be able to get away for our mixed doubles tournament?" Three months ago when we'd registered, who knew a murder investigation would interfere?

Russ grinned. "I never skirt a commitment."

No, he didn't. "I still understand if you need to forfeit."

"Thank you. I plan to win gold tomorrow."

Of course he did. Russ had to be the most goal-oriented person I knew. We played well together. We certainly had a chance to win our bracket.

"I'm going to have to pass on dinner tonight, though." Russ gestured toward the Crown Ballroom. "You'll be okay walking Gem?"

The dog tossed her head and stared Russ down. I hadn't had any trouble so far. "I'm sure she'll take me where she wants to go."

"That's the spirit." Russ scratched Gem. "Take care of her."

I wasn't sure if Russ was talking to Gem or me. I got his message loud and clear. The complexity of the attempted burglary likely involved many people. The line between good guy and bad wasn't going to be so clear. The true test would be how far they were willing to go to keep their secrets. No wonder my heart pounded as I left the room, glad I had a watchdog at my side.

CHAPTER 5

A detour to the ladies' room, to touch up my worse-for-wear appearance before visiting Isaac Samuels's Old Barkview Inn jewelry store, made sense. While Russ viewed mussed hair and water-spotted shoes as part of the package, fastidious Isaac Samuels would run for cover. In fact, in the five years I'd known him and his brother, Jacob, I'd never seen a hair out of place on either of them.

I nudged Gem's side with my knee as she blocked my entrance into the modern-conveniences-meets-Victorian-elegance bathroom. Not even a huff from Gem, which made me feel worse. No doubt I should've seen it coming. In all fairness, in all the years I'd been around Gem and Ariana, I'd never noticed the dog being overprotective. The president's Secret Service detail could take lessons. Sure, Gem had seemed diligent and alert at Ariana's side, but Ariana had never seemed caged.

Before I could apologize, Gem sniffed skyward, shook her head, and then moved aside. As if a threat hid in the gold trimmed room on the off chance I'd stop by. Why, then, did I feel more anxious? Because I didn't need or want a protector. I took care of myself. I always had. Even Russ knew better than to overstep.

One look in the gilt-edged mirror, and I wondered if Gem's goal had been to protect me from myself. Yikes! My wet-to-dry hair stuck straight out in clown-like fashion. How Gem just looked fluffier made me crazy.

While Gem stretched across the doorway, effectively blocking any entry or exit, I quickly patted and retied my tawny hair, splashed water on my face, and applied mauve lipstick. Thank goodness for quick-dry fabrics. My skirt and top looked country-club appropriate.

The dog pressed against my leg, her nose sniffling far and wide as we walked past the wood-paneled walls picturing famous Old Barkview Inn guests in full color and, sometimes, grainy old black-and-white photos, to the shops.

Samuels and Sons Fine Jewelry occupied prime real estate on the right just beyond the photo gallery. Although it was smaller than Gem's Palace, you'd think the elegant wood and glass jewelry cases tastefully displaying black Tahitian, golden, luminescent cream, and perfectly matched multicolored South Sea pearls would inspire awe, especially for a bling fanatic like me. Not so much, it turned out. The dark-haired, middle-aged man methodically Windexing the counter and muttering to the empty store made me consider a quick about-face. I could wait for backup.

He saw me about the same time I noticed a red light on his earbud. Isaac flushed as he disconnected his call. Although the tailored suit hid much, he still outweighed me by more than a little. No way he could've squeezed through the ceiling path, even if he could have stood the dust and grime.

I expected Gem to pause and sniff, not to block the door. I swear her ears poofed out like Yoda's and then folded back flat.

Her deep-throated *You're-guilty-of-something* growl affected my heart rate. In Gem's view, Isaac Samuels was somehow involved.

"Welcome, Miss Wright. I see you have Miss Gem." He retreated behind the nearest counter, wiping the spotless glass before stashing the spray bottle. Not that I blamed him. Gem had intimidation covered. "To what do I owe this pleasure?"

As if he didn't know. "I wanted to talk to you about the Shepard Diamond."

His furtive glance never left Gem. Although she'd stopped growling, her ears remained flat, making her angular face even more intimidating. "Forgive me. That dog does not like me."

That dog had a lie-detector sense that rivaled my own.

"I'm not sure how I can help," Isaac said.

Taking a page from Aunt Char's get-'em-talking interview playbook, I began. "I understand you were instrumental in influencing the Smithsonian to release the diamond for our exhibition."

"It is true. I caused Chris's death." His bowed head just added to the drama.

Give me a break. "I don't understand." Of course I did, but his explanation would be interesting. This man didn't have the temperament to be a crack shot with a dart gun. "How exactly did you kill him?"

"Not in the literal sense," he assured me too quickly. "If I hadn't convinced the Smithsonian to allow the loan, he would not have been in the room when the villains arrived."

"Villains?" I asked. "What makes you think there are more than one?"

His complexion paled. "I, uh, just assumed."

More to that story for sure. Something about the explanation didn't ring true. Could Isaac be protecting someone? Judging from his pressed lips, he knew he'd said too much. I went for another angle. “Why did you ask for the diamond to begin with?”

“Adam Smythe requested help. You know Samuels and Sons is well connected at the GIA. We are also contributors to the Smithsonian gemology department.”

Big contributors, apparently. “Why that diamond? The Hope Diamond would be a bigger draw.”

Isaac shrugged. “You will need to ask Adam. He asked and I delivered.”

“For a foothold in Barkview.” I gestured around me.

Isaac’s huff confirmed my suspicions. “Which begs the question, why did you want space here at the Old Barkview Inn? This does not have the foot traffic of Rodeo Drive.”

“Certainly not. I was promised far more.” His frustration seemed real enough.

I glanced at his sea-themed display. “Pretty.” Elegant, really. Not my style. “May I ask who your target audience is?”

Isaac sniffed. “We cater to upscale resort visitors.”

“Do you have any dog-related merchandise?”

“Certainly not. Barkview is a seaside resort.”

“Unbending” about summed up Isaac’s stance. And completely out of touch. “What were you promised?”

Isaac huffed again. He knew he’d said too much.

“It seems our previous mayor has a lot to answer for,” I said lightly.

“That he does.” No questioning the truth in that statement. Isaac reached behind the counter and handed me a Gem’s Palace jewelry box with a red bow. “Ariana requested I give this to you.”

I knew exactly what it was. The offered box still threw me off, and it took me a second to accept it. “I, uh, didn’t know you were friends.”

“Industry colleagues.”

On a good day. Ariana had to have been desperate. I opened the box. The German Shepherd charm with a multicolored stone collar for the charm bracelet she'd given me didn't surprise me, but the note tucked beneath tugged at my curiosity. "When did Ariana give this to you?"

"Wednesday. She said you'd be in to see me sometime this week with Gem."

So, Ariana had suspected something was going to happen even before the Shepard Diamond had arrived in Barkview. I thanked Isaac and left. I made it as far as the staircase to the lobby before reading the note. I'd hoped for a clue. Not a pearl of wisdom I didn't want to think about.

"Your journey continues, Cat. I can tell you men are a challenge. I do not regret my choices. Only you can decide if it is worth taking the chance."

No kidding. The men in my life embodied the word 'challenge.' A vision of my father's funeral swamped me. The twenty-one-gun salute and the flag folded in military precision. I saw Russ next. Not safely smiling on the beach, but hanging upside down from the Crown Ballroom ceiling, bullets flying around him. In some ways they were so alike. Was the risk of losing him worth it?

Somehow Gem's head ended up beneath my hand. Oddly, the feel of her soft fur comforted me. Why couldn't this case just be about a missing diamond?

CHAPTER 6

The clues in every investigation added up to something eventually, I reminded myself for the umpteenth time. Why did connecting the dots in this one seem so hopeless?

I glanced at Gem, copiloting my Jag, her head confidently high. If only self-assurance could be transferred. I exhaled and called Sandy as I drove south on First Street toward Adam Smythe's residence.

"What did you find out from Adam's assistant?" No doubt Sandy's disarming good looks and everybody's-best-friend persona had prompted the usual confidences.

"Either Ty is a total yes-man or a seriously gifted politician," Sandy replied.

Not the expected answer. Quite the compliment from Miss-I-know-everything. I pictured her jaw clenching in frustration. "What did he say?"

"It's what he didn't say that's so annoying."

He really had stumped her. Had to be a first. A good lesson that when good looks and charm fail, the real work began. "What did he say?"

“Only that Mayor Smythe’s late wife had a fascination with yellow diamonds.”

“Lynda Smythe flaunted South Sea pearls and a five-carat Smythe family wedding band.” I should know. Although Lynda had been murdered during the Cavalier dognappings, she and my aunt had shared a long rivalry. I wasn’t the only one who knew it, either.

“Doesn’t mean she didn’t like them. Ty said Mayor Smythe found a reference to the Douglas Diamond in Mrs. Smythe’s papers.” The excitement in Sandy’s voice resonated. After a long year reading countless diaries and tracking go-nowhere leads, any mention of the Barkview treasure resonated.

“What was it?”

“No idea. When I pressed him for specifics, he pleaded ignorance.”

“You believed him?”

“Yeah.”

I felt her frustration, too. That left us no closer to locating the Douglas Diamond than when Jan had died protecting it. “Did he really call Adam ‘Mayor Smythe?’”

“He did. I wanted to correct him, but it’s appropriate. ‘Former Mayor Smythe’ sounds so much better.”

No argument from me. Ty’s apparent loyalty did make me question his reliability.

“See what you can find out about Samuels and Sons Fine Jewelry and their relationship with Adam Smythe’s campaign, the GIA, and the Smithsonian. Isaac indicated he’d been promised more business than he’s gotten for the Old Barkview location.”

“Former mayor stretching the truth?” Sandy asked.

“Maybe.” There’d been a lot of that going around when Aunt Char took over.

“The justification for term limits,” Sandy said.

No argument from me. "Call Adam Smythe, too. Let him know I'll be at his house shortly. I have some information about Firebird Industries he'll want to hear."

Sandy choked on whatever she'd just sipped. "Oh, you're good. Go right for the man's money supply."

The prospect of being a trust fund baby without said fund did ensure a man fixated on appearances would at least see me. "Let's hope I can get him to talk. There's more to Adam pursuing the Shepard Diamond. I can feel it."

I disconnected the call as I turned into the circular driveway leading to the Smythe home. Built in the Spanish colonial style by a Smythe ancestor in 1946, the five-acre garden estate featured a two-story main house with a red barrel-tiled roof, a barn, a caretaker's cottage, and an unobstructed view of Bark Rock when clouds didn't blanket the shore in gray drizzle.

The rustic wood door blocked my entrance, a stark reminder of my last visit when the Smythes' Cavalier had been dognapped. Gem sniffed as she exited my SUV but did not object as I led her to the door.

Chelsea Smythe, Adam and Lynda's daughter, answered on the second ring. A younger version of her mother, Chelsea wore her dark hair in an elegant twist. Her black slacks, white-dotted cardigan, and soft leather loafers added up to class. Lady Mag, Lynda's champion Cavalier King Charles, hugged Chelsea's side.

Of course, Chelsea's once-over found me wanting. That she still blamed me for her mother's murder didn't surprise me. Not that I'd had any control over the outcome.

"I thought you'd gone back to San Francisco." Would Chelsea give up that dream job at a prestigious firm to stay in Barkview forever?

"Dad needs me." No smile. Just the facts.

No doubt she blamed me for him losing reelection as well. "I'm sorry." I really was. I related to family obligation far too well.

"Hi, Gem," Chelsea said. Gem dropped her head for a scratch with no hesitation or speculative sniffing.

How disappointing. I'd half-hoped she'd point to Adam as Chris's killer. Why did I feel betrayed? "Your father is expecting me."

"He cleared thirty minutes for you. Please follow me."

I should've felt honored, not annoyed as I followed her past the enormous vase filled with pink and white roses that dominated the foyer. Nothing had changed since my last visit. To the right, the formal portrait of Lady Mag, regally posed on Lynda's lap, still hung above the marble mantle.

Recognition struck when I entered a book-lined study overlooking the gardens. The room looked suspiciously like my aunt's mayoral office, right down to the ornate mahogany desk. Dressed in a Barkview Golf Club shirt and slacks with his salt-and-pepper hair neatly styled, Adam epitomized a country club gentleman. He offered me a chair under the air conditioning duct, no doubt selected to keep the meeting short.

"Coffee?" Chelsea asked.

I nodded. I smelled the Woofing Best dark roast as the hot liquid kissed my cup. Chelsea added caramel flavoring without asking. Was I that predictable?

I wrapped my fingers around the mug, hoping the warmth would halt my knee knocking. Chelsea handed her father another cup and took the seat beside me.

Adam didn't give me a minute to get situated. "What do you think you know, Cat?"

Any question this meeting hadn't been staged disappeared. Despite the short notice, he'd anticipated my visit. Good thing zero pleasantries suited me just fine. "I know your family's construction company rebuilt the Old Barkview Inn's Crown Ballroom ceiling twelve inches lower than the city drawings show."

Adam shared a conspiratorial glance with Chelsea. They were hiding something, all right.

"What does that have to do with me? My uncles are all deceased, and the family sold the business to Firebird Industries ten years ago," Adam replied.

No denial. "I need to see your uncles' files on the Old Barkview Inn."

Chelsea chimed in, "All the architectural files were turned over to the new owners at sale. The law only requires drawings to be kept for fifteen years."

"The Old Barkview Inn refurbishment was forty years ago," Adam added.

I sat back. "You don't expect me to believe you destroyed Barkview history or relinquished those files. Where are the original drawings?"

"You don't need to answer that, Dad."

Adam crossed his arms, unmoving. So much for cooperation.

"This is a simple request," I said. "Your refusal to cooperate is making me wonder what you are hiding."

Adam's sudden chuckle made me gnash my teeth. "I am hiding nothing. All documents related to the Old Barkview Inn are public records and housed in the City Hall archives. Anyone who wants to can access them Monday through Friday during business hours."

I really should've known it was that simple. Was my inherent Adam Smythe distrust affecting my judgment?

"So, that's how Chris Papas broke in," Adam said. "You know, he asked Ty for the 1890s drawings about a year ago."

Chelsea admiring her manicure at that moment wasn't a coincidence.

"Did you ask why?"

"He claimed he needed the exact proportions to design a piece of jewelry, probably for your aunt." Who else would Adam throw blame on?

Truth or exaggeration? His flippancy made it hard to tell. "Isn't that when Samuels and Sons started construction on their store at the Old Barkview Inn?"

"As a matter of fact, I believe you are correct. Isaac should be pleased his store was spared a break-in."

Or not. "Perhaps he would prefer an insurance payoff." I hadn't meant to suggest that out loud. Maybe I had. Chelsea sat taller. She really was her mother's daughter.

"He's not happy with his sales?" Adam asked smoothly. "I told him Gem's Palace was a Barkview institution."

Isaac's inventory also needed review. In my humble opinion, anyway. "Yet you took his money and influence."

"Politics, my dear." He shared a glance with Chelsea. "I did warn him. My daughter would say I provided full disclosure of the challenges. He insisted his reputation would prevail."

Arrogance did not make for a sound business plan. "Isaac indicated otherwise."

"Not from me."

I wasn't sure why, but I believed him. Who else would Isaac take advice from?

"Why did you want the Shepard Diamond for the gala?" I asked.

Another shared look between father and daughter. "I didn't. Lynda did."

No dodge. No dance. Just a nonchalant response that begged me to ask, "Why?"

"My wife believed the Douglas Diamond is also a fancy yellow."

My turn to stare. "Are you telling me your deceased wife was a Douglas Diamond hunter?"

"Hardly. She'd never risk mussing her manicure," Adam said.

That sounded more like the woman I remembered.

"Lynda believed that the Shepard Diamond and the Douglas Diamond were related," Adam explained.

Lynda was smarter than that. "Related how? Diamonds don't have familial DNA."

"They do if they are cut from the same larger stone," Chelsea said.

True, but... "That would have to be at least a fifty- or sixty-carat fancy yellow."

"You do know your diamonds. Her notes referenced a sixty-five-carat fancy yellow and then twin eighteen-carat stones in 1918."

That year marked the end of World War I and the breakup of the powerful German states. The Spanish flu. The fall of imperial Russia. The beginning of European involvement in South African diamond mines. Where would a previously unknown sixty-five-carat yellow diamond come from? As if I couldn't venture a guess.

"And bringing the Shepard Diamond to Barkview would make the Douglas Diamond reveal itself?" I asked. It made no sense.

Chelsea's head shake showed she agreed with me on that. "Not entirely logical."

Not typical behavior for a practical woman, either. Someone had convinced her to believe it to help orchestrate a diamond theft. If the Douglas and Shepard Diamonds really were part of one whole and someone wanted them back together... Why? The stones were pretty. A matching pair would be worth upward of twenty million dollars. A significant amount of money, for sure, but not world-changing value-wise.

"How did Lynda learn about the link between the Shepard and Douglas Diamonds?" I asked Adam.

"I don't know. After my wife's death, I read some of her private papers."

I felt like the cat staring at the canary cage, especially when Chelsea stood, indicating my time had expired.

Curiosity clawed at me, but I recognized a wall when I saw it, and I quietly followed Chelsea out. That I'd been royally manipulated didn't bother me half as much as wondering why they'd toyed with me about Lynda's private documents.

Had they tried to find the Douglas Diamond and failed? Then why involve me? So far, I'd failed too. Maybe my intuition had been right all along. Finding the stone mattered less than discovering where it came from and why someone would kill for it.

CHAPTER 7

Leaving the Smythes' house with more questions than answers, I knew I needed Sandy's computer skills. A plan in mind, I called in an order and detoured to the Sit and Stay Café to pick up bribery burgers. Today rain dripped from the quaint green-gabled Craftsman, sending the usual veranda patrons indoors. In all fairness, the handful of people weren't the problem. The mountain of a Saint Bernard blockading the entry was. No way Gem and I could pass side by side. The dog fixed the problem. She paused, allowing me to sidestep the hairy heap to access the reception podium.

Dressed in a red bolero jacket and white blouse that accented her dark good looks, Nell met me at the marble-topped counter, while Blur, her lovable black Labrador Retriever, dropped a tennis ball at my feet. Call it jealousy or, more likely, pride, but Gem filled the space between us so fast I didn't have a chance to even reach for the ball.

"Welcome to you, too, Gem." While amusement laced Nell's words, Blur's evil eye incited a head toss from the Shepherd.

Me, mediate a dog fight? Before this could get out of hand, I said, “Yum. That smells good.” I wasn’t kidding either. The aroma of the two sirloin burgers and battered fries made my mouth water. Why had I ordered a chicken salad for me? Of course, I’d steal a few French fries, but the way Gem licked her lips, Sandy would have a battle for that second burger.

“I figured you had custody of Gem when I saw your order,” Nell said.

It had to be some cosmic joke that I seemed to end up caring for jailbirds’ dogs. I didn’t need to look to know Gem had attached herself to my side like a permanent appendage. Didn’t she ever take a break? What kind of danger could I possibly be in next door to police headquarters?

Nell took a burger from the bag and offered it to Gem. “What are you doing?” Sandy would kill me.

“Aren’t these for Gem?” Nell seemed genuinely confused. “She’s a total burger-monster. Cheese and extra mayo.”

“No. They’re for Sandy. What about the fries?”

“Figured they were for you.”

Which made sense, considering my just-one-fry tendencies. Gem didn’t want the burger anyway. Although she fixated on the meaty mess, she didn’t make a move toward it.

“You need to give her permission,” Nell explained.

“For what?” I glanced at the dog’s proud profile. Gem did whatever she wanted.

“She won’t take food without your permission,” Nell insisted.

That made zero sense to my mind, even with my limited experience with dogs. “Why not?” Renny inhaled anything and everything within tongue range. Bayle, Rayelle’s Bichon Frise, had been slightly different, but he still ate anything in his bowl. What was Gem’s deal?

“Someone could try to poison her to get to you. You need to

tell her she can eat the food first," Nell said. "You know that Gem is a well-trained guard dog, right?"

"Don't remind me." My shins ached from our daylong positioning struggles.

"Feeling a tad confined?"

"Not funny. Seriously, you have no idea." Not entirely true. Nell ran two successful businesses, cared for her aging parents, and managed a nationally-ranked flyball team. She got responsibility.

"Okay. I'll quit. Just stop torturing her," Nell said.

Who was torturing who here? "What do I do?"

"Tell her it's okay to eat it," Nell suggested.

It couldn't be that simple, not the way my week had been going. "Go ahead. It's okay," I said, gesturing toward the burger. I swear Gem rolled her eyes. Of course there was a specific command. Wouldn't she get tired of waiting and...?

Gem just blinked at me, her look impatient. Censured by a dog. Story of my life.

"Try saying 'Eat,'" Nell suggested.

I did. Not even a stutter step. Obviously, Gem did eat. I just needed to know the proper words. What words would Ariana use? "*Bon appétit*," I said. Still nothing.

"It could be anything," Nell said.

No kidding. Considering Ariana's German heritage, the command could easily not even be in English. I had no choice. I texted Uncle G. He responded right away. He didn't type "Duh," but I felt it after I read his response. "Take it," I said.

Of course, Gem carefully removed the burger from Nell's hand and gobbled it in three bites. No wonder the dog had indigestion.

Nell smiled. "That makes sense."

Only to a dog person. I took the paper bags from Nell.

"KDOG is doing a piece on Lynda Smythe's contribution to Barkview." I ignored my friend's raised brows. "It's time."

"A peace offering isn't a bad thing," Nell suggested.

So that was the way of it. Ineffective as Mayor Smythe had been, public opinion sided with the lonely widower. If they only knew the mess Aunt Char still worked through daily. I bit back my retort. I really hated politics. "I understand she worked with children's groups."

"Donated to them, you mean. Trust me when I tell you her best contribution was financial." Nell should know. She headed the Barkview Kids Training Dogs program, which recruited children to train therapy dogs.

"Her daughter seems to be following in her heels."

"Same type A personality with less polish," Nell said. "Don't get me wrong. I appreciate Chelsea's enthusiasm."

"Just not her interference."

"Exactly. The girl has too much time on her hands."

I knew that. "Who did Lynda pal around with?" Lynda and my aunt's rivalry made me persona non grata in her world.

"Far as I know, she kept to herself. It was no secret she ran City Hall. Gabby would be a better source. Lynda did like her café mochas."

No need to add that Gabby excelled at gabbing. I thanked Nell and motioned Gem to follow.

"Gem is a working dog. You'll need to force her to play," Nell advised me.

How was I supposed to force a determined German Shepherd to do anything?

As if on cue, Nell's black Labrador Retriever nudged her hand for a head scratch. The lab might as well have purred, the way she contorted so Nell would get the right spot. Who said dogs weren't manipulators?

Since Gabby worked the early morning shift, I did not

detour to the Daily Wag but drove west on Sycamore to Second Street and turned right into the KDOG studio parking lot. Located a block off the Barkview beach, the two-story light-blue and white gingerbread-trimmed Victorian enjoyed ocean views from the second-floor executive offices. I parked in my designated spot beside Aunt Char's and took Gem in the employee entrance.

I found Sandy in the phone booth we called a studio control room, completing the preshow sound check. Maybe not the best timing since my aunt's dog psychiatry show, *Throw Him a Bone*, aired in forty minutes.

"I brought dinner." I held up the burger bag.

As usual, Sandy took my arrival in stride, masking any annoyance behind enthusiasm. "I can forgive anything for extra jalapenos."

I knew that too well, actually, and handed her the burger bag. "There were two," I said, frowning in Gem's direction. No way Gem could've understood, but her tongue licked her lips.

Sandy ripped open the bag, took out the burger, and laid out the fries just the way I liked them. She ripped off a fourth of the burger and offered it to Gem. "Take it." Gem swallowed the piece whole.

Of course, Sandy knew the command. "How did you know?"

Sandy stroked Gem's head. "I asked Ariana. Did you know Gem's a trained guard dog?"

No kidding, and I was her current project. That she'd been trained to be this way shocked me. Had Ariana really been so frightened living in Barkview all these years? "Did you ever wonder why?"

Sandy frowned. "I figured Ariana was concerned about the jewelry store. Chris traveled a lot. I never imagined how deep her secrets were."

Okay. I felt better.

Sandy got right to business. "Samuels and Sons Jewelry is now owned by the two Samuels sons, one ex-wife, and a private equity company." Sandy bit into the remainder of the burger. "Apparently, the company ran into some financial troubles recently and sold forty percent of the stock six months ago."

"Don't tell me the ex-wife's share can sway the majority."

"Great planning, huh?" Sandy took another long, satisfying burger-bite. How she remained so trim made me crazy. I glanced at a burger and gained weight. "The interesting part is that the private equity company owns mostly commercial real estate in mid-range markets. Samuels and Sons is their first retail venture."

"A mid-range-specific property company buying into a high-end jewelry store?" I asked.

"I know, strange, huh?"

My thoughts exactly. "Money talks. Especially in the light of desperation."

"The Smithsonian connection isn't so easy to track. What I know is Isaac or Jacob brokered a deal for a client to donate two rare minerals to the national collection. Despite what Isaac claims, that wasn't what secured the Shepard Diamond for Barkview's exhibition."

"Who was the collector?"

"Officially anonymous."

Not impossible to discover, just more challenging, I reminded myself.

"Your GIA or FBI liaison might know more. They are a tight-lipped group." Poor Sandy, thwarted by Ty and now the Smithsonian. She had to wonder if she was losing her touch.

"How does our former mayor fit into all this?" Somehow he

did. I could feel it. At least my intuition was speaking to me again. Maybe I was getting closer.

"I'll leave that to you to figure out," Sandy said. "When was the last time you took Gem out?"

I frowned. "We've been out all day. Why?"

"Poor thing is crossing her legs," Sandy said.

"What?" Gem sat on guard between me and the door. "I don't understand..." But I did. I needed to walk her. "Why didn't she tell me?" Renny barked at the door or yanked me toward the grass.

"She has. You're not paying attention to her."

What? I couldn't seem to read Gem. "What should I be looking for?"

"See how close she is to the door?"

"She's always between me and the door."

"She's nosing the doorknob."

"Nosing?" Okay, maybe Gem was closer to the door, but the control room was closet-sized.

"I'm guessing there's a bell in the bag I gave you. Hang it on your doorknob at home. She'll ring it when she wants to go out," Sandy said.

"A bell?" That was a good idea for someone with no doggie door. I'd struggled with Bayle when he'd stayed with me.

"Gem will bark once when she wants to come back inside. Listen for it."

Hard to miss a big dog's bark. Although ten years had passed since the Pit Bull attack that put me in the hospital, I still gnashed my teeth around big dogs. "I thought Gem knew how to open doors herself." Ariana bragged about that often enough.

Sandy thought about it a second before responding. "I think she can open the flat handle on interior doors. Not sure if it's even possible to open a round doorknob with paws," Sandy said. "I wouldn't take a chance when she needs to go out."

Neither would I. Gem letting herself out would be a bonus. The thought of Gem opening my bedroom door and strolling in at will kind of creeped me out. "You understand Gem." I meant it too. "She should be with you."

"She's your journey, Cat. I've discovered mine."

True. Not sure who'd chosen who in that Jack Russell Terrier relationship. "You're starting to sound like Ariana."

"Hardly. You're the investigator. I'm the behind-the-computer girl."

Who knew everything and everyone. "What else did Ariana say to do?" Better late than never to ask.

"Play with Gem. She chases balls to relax."

Why didn't that surprise me? No couch potato here.

"She should do well in the Fetch-a-thon Pickleball Tournament in the morning," Sandy added.

Just my luck they'd rescheduled the dogs' event for tomorrow. To honor the pickleball legend that cofounder Joel Pritchard's dog, Pickles, regularly stole the game ball, Barkview scheduled an opening game free-for-all during which four players dinked on center court while dogs tried to interrupt. The first dog to retrieve the ball won the coveted Pickle Ball, a golden pickleball most people considered more prestigious than the players' medals.

"If we play," I said.

"It stopped raining hours ago, and the fans are blow-drying the courts. There's talk they'll reschedule the pro matches, but the women's events had to be canceled. You and Russ will crush the mixed-doubles event tomorrow. I know it."

I smiled. I couldn't help myself. We did play oddly well together. Most couples fought over center court ball hogging or poor shot selection. Not us. We seemed to read and anticipate one another's moves well on and off the court.

"You know, they say the couple who plays pickleball together..." Sandy's wink made me blush.

"Get divorced." I would've stuck my tongue out at her too, but Gem took that moment to let one rip. Not a delicate little fluffy fart, but a 3rd-Marine-Division toot that smelled so bad that Sandy and I rushed out of the control room for air. Big gulps of it.

"My nose hairs are burned out," Sandy complained.

"Gem's double-cheese-and-mayonnaise-burger days are over," I announced. No wonder the dog had stomach issues.

Aunt Char and Renny strolled onto the set, saving us from a deeper analysis. I exited. No need for me to micromanage Sandy. I'd trained her well. Better than Aunt Char had trained me to take over the general manager's position when she'd moved to City Hall. No doubt it was the pupil. Frankly, I'd traded hair-graying chaos for mountains of paperwork and programming disputes. No wonder I'd jumped on a new investigation. I felt alive again. I suddenly got why Aunt Char wanted to continue her show despite her mayoral duties.

CHAPTER 8

When you live in a world of rings, pings, and dings, a bell on the doorknob is a sleep-preventing, jump-at-any-sound long night. Not that Gem wanted out. She just lay at the door, guarding me from forces known only to her, one eye on my every toss and turn. I guess I felt both super-safe and stifled at the same time.

No wonder that when the 7 a.m. alarm fired, I woke with a start and a splitting headache. Before both my eyes even opened, I fumbled for my phone. Of course, Russ, the ever-ready-rooster-rouser, had already texted. Our pickleball match was on, and yes, we started in two hours. No time to roll over and restart. I tripped over the vacant dog bed as I stumbled to my feet, just as the telltale bell tolled.

Furballs! Ariana's no-dallying warning about Gem needing to go out came front and center. My leopard-print PJs with the lace trim weren't exactly public attire, but the second ring, more insistent than the first, made me drop my toothbrush and meet Gem, leash in her mouth, at the door.

In my haste, I even bypassed the coffeemaker as Gem

dragged me right out the door. Outside, the morning mist felt like cold water on my face and broke through my stupor. With any luck, the visibility-limiting fog would also reduce the number of walkers. Just maybe I could get the job done unnoticed. Seriously, if not for the surf rolling onto the shore, I'd wonder where the beach had gone.

Gem sniffed skyward and then headed south on the boardwalk, the grassy park her goal. I double-stepped to keep pace. No need to rush her: two steps on the damp grass soaking through my slippers and she did her business—a mountain of it compared to a Cavalier and a Bichon, and the smell... Ugh. I needed an industrial-grade shovel. Great Dane owners had my sympathy.

I took a critical look at the poo pile. Color: dark brown. No green grass or corn kernels or anything else recognizable sticking out of it. Steam wafted off it. Was that normal? Obsessing over doggie do had to stop. In all fairness, the last thing I needed was a constipated, endlessly farting dog.

I looked around. For every small-dog-approved poop-bag dispenser around town, there ought to be a corresponding shovel stop too. This was big-dog discrimination. Okay. I admit it. I was procrastinating.

The handful of dogs and their walkers milling in the park killed any hope for a quick escape. I ripped a bag out of the leash dispenser, slipped my hand in, held my breath, and went for it. Bigger than a handful, I had a two-bag job here. I grabbed the first mound. The actual heat of it shocked me, but not as much as its gooey, squishy feel between my fingers and oozing under my fingernails. I gagged as I pulled the plastic edge over the pile and lifted... the bag right off my hand! OMG! The poo still stuck to my palm.

My scream jammed in my hyperventilating throat as I

panic-flicked my hand, flinging dog do every which way. Ick! Ick! It clung to me like fossilized glue.

Suddenly, a white wet-wipe blocked out the whole mess. Russ's sneeze announced his arrival even before his words. "Breathe, Cat."

Breathe? I'd been sucked into the yuck-vacuum.

"Come on, Cat. In and out. That's right."

I obeyed, skip-breathing until another sneeze broke the Zen and I felt every eye in the park boring into me as if I'd lost my mind. Okay. Maybe I had overreacted a tad. I blushed. So much for stealth.

Russ took Gem's leash from me and handed me a Woofing Best coffee cup. The caramel cappuccino aroma wrapped around me in a warm hug.

"What happened?" he asked.

As if he didn't know. "Gem's poo melted the bags." A good reason never to use the green biodegradable ones, for sure.

"Melted?" A grin sneaked through his seriousness.

I crossed my arms. "I swear..."

"I believe you. Really." He inspected another bag. Naturally, it fit his hand perfectly. No holes. He tried another with the same results.

"They're defective," I insisted.

"Okay. I believe you."

He didn't, but humoring me was okay too. "We'll get you a personal pooper-scooper this afternoon."

"You mean they actually have those?"

"Yeah. You don't need to touch a thing."

I was going to kill Sandy for this. Surely, she knew about the pooper-scooper thingy. On second thought, I quickly surveyed my surroundings. It would be just like her to plant a camera... but there was no sign of mischief.

Russ showed me an industrial-size pooper-scooper on his

phone. The shovel-like dual-claw base looked easy enough to use. "How do you know about this stuff?" I asked. "Your mom's Portuguese Water Dog doesn't need a shovel."

His grin drew mine. "I saw a guy with two Great Danes using one and asked."

Twin pooping-machine dogs? I'd run away.

"Amazon reviews give it 4.5 stars." Russ tapped his screen. "It'll be at your place tomorrow."

Until then... Russ saved me from the dirty duty when he pulled a fresh bag from his pocket. What non–dog owner carried poop bags? Especially in tennis shorts and a freshly pressed polo? Yes, the man did iron them.

I sipped my coffee, a sense of unreality coming over me as he bagged the scattered poop. He'd saved the day again. "Thank you."

"You're welcome. We need to check in in less than an hour. I'll finish walking Gem. Go home and get ready."

Me, give myself an extra fifteen minutes in the a.m.? Never. He knew me too well. I hugged him anyway, suddenly concerned that he wasn't part of the Gem pack. Would she even go with him?

Clearly, Gem didn't like it one bit, but the hug helped and Russ handled her. So well, in fact, that she stood in majestic pride beside him. A bigger dog suited him. I couldn't think about that now. I'd freaked out over nothing. No doubt Aunt Char had already heard about it.

She'd laugh, but I'd put her in another embarrassing situation. Politics! Would I ever get used to the endless scrutiny?

Russ and Gem arrived as I put Gem's food out. The ripe, meaty smell made me gag. No wonder Gem had bathroom problems. Nothing a quick stop at Chef Rayelle's Barkery couldn't solve. As usual, she sniffed every crevice in the house before returning to the kitchen to sit in front of her bowl. She waited for my command before eating. Russ waved away the yogurt I offered him.

"Gem's a pleasure," he said. I swear the dog winked at him. Another smitten female.

"I agree. You should take her..."

"Don't go there, Cat. I will help when I can."

I wanted to stamp my feet. "Ariana put you up to this, didn't she?" The woman had an agenda. I just knew it.

"You really believe that?" Russ asked.

"No." I really didn't. Russ kowtowed to no one.

"I have a professional conflict here."

"Because Ariana is convinced Gem will find the diamond and Chris's killer?" I asked.

"Because my company is potentially liable in this case. Even the appearance of impropriety will affect the prosecution."

I knew that, but it didn't make the big-dog adjustment any easier. I exhaled, resigned. This insanely protective dog and I were partners until I found the Shepard Diamond.

CHAPTER 9

Gem and I arrived at pickleball check-in with only minutes to spare. Who knew parking would be so tight? I'd nixed carpooling with Russ. He couldn't play well today if he was wheezing.

I swear Gem shed a fur coat everywhere she went. Not single hairs either, but black-and-tan puffs that floated like a fluff cyclone. Outdoors Russ stood a chance, but not even Celeste Barklay's famed allergy pills would help if he was confined in a car with Gem. I couldn't think about the residual allergy issues in my house right now either.

A trip to the Fluff and Buff salon could only help. Michelle Le Fleur always had a helpful dog-grooming tip or ten.

Russ sneezed as he took my pickleball bag and handed me my neon first-server wristband. "We start on court six immediately following the Fetch-a-thon. News is, the Romas forfeited their rescheduled mixed-double pro match. Loreli is still participating in the charity fetch."

"That's a shame. I would have enjoyed watching their split-court style up close." Logan basically played singles, diving all over the court, while Loreli stayed out of his way. In all fairness, her defensive resets were worthy of a how-to video, and she didn't need to do much else for the team to win.

"Rumor has it he banged up his forearm in a surfing mishap yesterday afternoon," Russ explained.

Curious timing. "He went surfing in a storm the day before a high-stakes match?" I asked. "Which arm?" According to Ariana, Gem had bitten her taller attacker.

"A good question. Could be a coincidence."

Except Russ didn't believe in them. And physically, Logan's tall, thin frame did match Ariana's description of one attacker. Who'd ever have suspected a professional pickleball player's involvement?

I winked at Russ as I led the way to the center-court bark-fest. Leads did come from random places. Although Gem heeled perfectly, an underlying excitement added a prance to her step. Was I starting to understand this dog?

She couldn't possibly know what was happening. Could she? The yipping, yapping, and woofing took me right back to Bayle's flyball match a few months ago. At least that event had ended well. Why didn't I feel lucky this time?

Gem's eyes seemed to sparkle when we arrived at the converted three-tier tennis stadium. The regulation badminton-sized pickleball court allowed for wider side lines, now packed shoulder to shoulder with a motley assortment of sleek, agile dogs; fluffy, ornamental dogs; and poised flyball champions. Dressed in everything from Bow Wow Boutique's chic running suits to basic leather collars, the contenders all crouched at the ready.

Gem steered me right to Sandy, who'd staked out a spot at the no-volley zone line. I slipped in beside her Jack Russell Terrier, bouncing like a rubber ball at her side.

The four pickleball pros, two men and two women, stood

at their respective baselines, paddles up, prepared to take on the dogs in their wild keep-away race to the ball. I had to admire their determination. The dogs invariably snatched the ball midair before the first bounce. With Aunt Char, the ribbon-cutting-queen, tossing the ball into play, I figured any one of the many Frisbee champs would pinch the ball before it made it past mid-court.

At least my aunt looked good decked out in St. John casual, with Renny holding Cavalier court on her right side, seemingly bored with the whole show.

Aunt Char winked at me and began speaking: "Now that we are all here..."

I blushed. So much for sneaking in unnoticed. My aunt continued to thank everyone for attending and introduced the four participating pros. Although I'd seen photos of Loreli Roma, in person the athletic superstar seemed shorter and more petite than I expected. Ariana had said one of her attackers had been taller and the other smaller. Could it have been the Romas? Despite Logan's suspicious injury, I doubted their involvement since Gem hadn't given Loreli a second glance.

Sandy tapped me on the shoulder. "Ready?"

Oh, yeah. I refocused.

Aunt Char continued. "Our generous professionals are convinced their surefire strategy will prevail and will donate one hundred dollars for each time the ball crosses the net to our Barkview Dog Shelter. In the spirit of competition and a new puppy wing, I challenge you all to match their generosity and donate as well." A smart political move on Aunt Char's part. Now no one wanted the dogs to win immediately.

Except Nell. I heard her before I saw her at the baseline, obscured by her lab, Blur. "Who will donate a hundred dollars for a first-hit catch?"

Sandy photographed the challenge acceptors. "Where's Ty?" I asked. Aunt Char's mayoral assistant should be recording the event.

"Sick in bed. Nell delivered her guaranteed-to-get-you-back-on-your-feet chicken soup to his place last night and said he looked like a ghost. Mrs. B is sending Doc White over tomorrow if he doesn't perk up."

MIA for my aunt's biggest event to date? Was it simple bad timing or some hidden agenda? No need to worry. Aunt Char had it covered. Ty would either be back tomorrow or under Doc White's oh-so-diligent care.

The donations recorded, Aunt Char displayed the neon-yellow pickleball. "Ladies and gentlemen, unleash your competitors." The simultaneous leash clicks sounded like one big floodgate opening. "Let the Fetch-a-thon begin."

Instead of tossing the ball, Aunt Char bounced it in front of Renny, who swatted it directly to Loreli on the east-facing side. She leaned low and lobbed the ball skyward, so high I had to shade my eyes to see it cross the net. Twenty or so dogs darted onto the court, tangling together, barking a crescendo. So much for an out-of-the-box dog win.

After the first return, they just stood there bobbleheaded, their many jeweled collars creating a rainbow across the court as their heads followed each high lob. From elaborate J Tracker pavé diamonds to chunky multicolored stones, the variety and scope of the bling display drew my eye. Natural or fake? Did it matter?

I smothered a smile. While Jack had taken off like the bullet he was, Gem remained at my side, her head following the ball. Was she waiting for a command or an opening? I couldn't tell until she crouched, her rear paws vibrating beneath her, waiting for the sixth return. Suddenly, she surged onto the court, jumping high enough to clear a six-foot fence, and caught the pickleball at its arc, snatching it a split second before it could strike Loreli's paddle and brushing her cheek with her fluffy German Shepherd tail. Loreli's screech stopped the applause mid-clap. Not that I blamed her. Being blindsided by an attack dog would send me back to therapy.

Gem landed in one fluid motion and trotted to Aunt Char's side. My aunt accepted the ball and placed the gold medal around the dog's neck. Her ears twitched at the praise. What could I say? Execution flawless. With any luck it portended Russ and my mixed-doubles performance on the pickleball courts.

Not so much, it turned out. We lost a three-game battle in round three and moved into the consolation bracket. Not Russ's fault. His deep returns and poaching should've carried us, but I lost concentration when Gem growled at Loreli and her tricolor Cavalier as they observed from the sidelines. Was Loreli as squeaky-clean as I'd originally assumed? Something about her proud posture and classic European looks seemed familiar. I just couldn't place it.

Russ saw my wandering attention right away and tried to refocus me. Too bad I dinked three balls straight into the net first. Ugh! It's always the easy shot. There were days I really hated this game.

Russ shrugged it off. "Your strategy just might pay off. We'll play fewer points per match to get to the gold medal round this way."

True. Playing one first-to-fifteen-point game did theoretically require winning fewer points to advance to the final round, but allowed no room for error.

Altogether, we played seven teams to reach the gold medal final match and ultimately played the team we'd lost to third round for the top honor. We won the match in three grueling games, but lost the tiebreaker to take home a silver medal. Not a bad outcome for our first tournament playing together, according to Russ. The man deserved double keeper points for that statement, for sure.

Naturally, Gem had to show off. Between the sparkling gold medal and her multi-jeweled collar, the bling about blinded us in the peekaboo afternoon sunlight. Did Swarovski crystals have that much depth or fire? Russ acknowledged my questioning gaze. It couldn't be that easy...

CHAPTER 10

It wasn't. We rushed through the medal ceremony to get Gem back to my place, where I dissected her collar and leash one stone at a time on my granite kitchen counter while she entered every room, checking for who knew what. In between Russ's sneezing fits, I louped every stone, even testing for a color sleeve on the larger, more likely yellow stone. No Shepard Diamond. Just a blingaholic's dream laid out on the fluffy white bath towel and a pea-size black tracker that looked more like a harmless tick than a threat.

Russ recognized it right away. "It's a basic untraceable model. Functional for a few months."

Was someone keeping tabs on Ariana or Chris? "Could Ariana have put it in?" The black dot had to be cheaper than paying the service fee on the J Tracker GPS collar my aunt's dog wore.

"Bug a dog that never leaves her side?"

There was that. "I know it sounds weird. Maybe it was just a precaution in Gem's case. People bug their dogs all the time.

Just look at how successful J Tracker's GPS collars are." I still had a hard time wrapping my mind around the concept.

"I'll have the chief ask her. The question is, why would anyone else want to track the dog?" Russ asked.

Good question. Gem shadowed Ariana, not Chris. Unless someone wanted to keep tabs on Ariana. I glanced at the dog protecting me from whoever thought about walking through my front door, her neck conspicuously naked. I'd Humpty-Dumptied that collar for sure. Too late to purchase a Bow Wow Boutique replacement today. When Russ located a plain leather collar in Gem's travel bag, I felt played. Ariana's insistence that Chris would hide the diamond in plain sight had led me to tear apart Gem's collar. Had that been the plan? Where else would he hide the Shepard Diamond?

I took a deep breath. Other than the Old Barkview Inn, where else had Chris been in the past week? Time to go back to basics and retrace his steps. No easy task in a town without outdoor surveillance cameras.

Russ heavy-poured two shiraz-du-jours and motioned me toward the patio. No complaint about the cool, offshore marine layer tonight. Russ needed air. I followed, brushing another fur blizzard off his back. How much fur could one dog shed and not have bald spots, anyway?

I picked more stubborn fuzz off my sleeve. "Max and Maxine don't shed this much." Celeste Barklay's allergy pills generally controlled Russ's sneezing around Uncle G's deputized German Shepherds. What was the difference?

Russ sniffled. "It's not just Gem's fur that's bothering me." He sneezed in emphasis. "It's her dander or saliva."

TMI. As if the pesky, light-as-air scales weren't bad enough, now there was dog spit in my car too?

"Hey. Don't panic, Cat. Gem's excessive shedding is probably stress related," Russ explained. "She's had a rough couple of days."

She wasn't the only one. His laissez-faire attitude helped calm me. If he could suffer with sneezing and itchy eyes, I could deal with the walking and corralling. "What do we do next?"

We'd made it to the sliding door when Gem answered that one for me with a clear-the-room fart that worked better than the bell ring.

"Geez, this is worse than the bomb she dropped in the studio." We both covered our noses and winced. How did Gem's sensitive nose not fall off?

"Do you want to walk Gem or grill the chicken?" Russ asked.

I opted for the walk. Sure, exercise could never hurt, but the clock ticked for solving Chris's murder. Walking a dog wasted valuable time. Why couldn't Gem be trained to use a toilet? She did everything else.

CHAPTER 11

I dropped Gem at the Fluff and Buff at 9 a.m. sharp for a full bath and pull-every-loose-hair brush. Michelle Le Fleur met me at the door with a European air-kiss. A Parisian by birth, Michelle's Champs-Élysées flair had taken Barkview's salon scene by storm about six years ago. Today her black smock with a gold logo covered basic black pants and a cap-sleeve top. A matching beret dipped smartly on her poodle-poofed hair.

"*Mon chérie*, felicitations on your gold medal." Her left-handed wave included Fifi, her jet-black, Standard French Poodle look-alike.

Michelle continued before I could correct her. "Your silver too, *Chat*."

You'd think I'd get it by now. Dogs always came first in Barkview. "Thank you for squeezing me in." I'd shamelessly used my Aunt Char's connection to bypass the three-week wait for an appointment. One Barklay Cavalier wouldn't get groomed this week. The puppy would thank me.

"Poor Monsieur Hawl. Allergic to dogs? I cannot imagine. I will triple-wash Mademoiselle Gem," Michelle promised.

That had to be better than a single wash, right?

"You will pick her up by noon. I am no Gem-sitter."

I nodded. Even I recognized a nonnegotiable order. Just because I'd used her grooming appointments as a dog-sitting service in the past didn't mean I would again. I blushed. Maybe I would. A few hours' reprieve from being under Gem-watch was appealing.

Gem growled at me when I handed Michelle her leash. Really? Michelle groomed the dog monthly. Not another elusive command. I pointed at Michelle. "Go, Gem."

Ugh. Her front paws locked; there'd be no moving her now. I couldn't place another call to Uncle G. Inspired, I embraced Michelle and said, "Gem, good." This replicated my introduction from Ariana too many hours ago to count anymore.

Gem looked me up and down and then moved to Michelle's side. A lottery win couldn't feel any better. I'd done something right. I scratched Gem's head, automatically swishing aside a fur puff.

Next stop, the Bow Wow Boutique for a new jeweled collar. Although Michelle hadn't remarked about Gem's generic collar, she'd wanted to, I could tell.

Michelle had more to say. "*C'est* sad about Monsieur Papas."

I inched toward the exit.

"I came to Barkview to be safe," Michelle declared.

That got my attention. I paused. "You don't feel safe?" Really? Where else did folks not even lock racked bikes?

"Monsieur Papas, Monsieur Looc, and Madame Smythe, all dead."

Yes, but... Michelle continued without waiting for a response. "Madame Smythe warned me to beware of change."

How draconian. "Change is never easy," I said diplomatically. "What did Lynda say about this change?"

"Only that Madame Orr told her to beware."

"Madame Orr?" Barkview's colorful Romani fortuneteller advertised herself as a psychic.

"*Mais oui.*" Michelle's nod sent the possibilities flying. What could Madame Orr and practical, politically savvy Lynda possibly have in common? "Are you sure Lynda consulted Madame Orr?"

"*Oui.* She waited until Lady Mag went to the rinse-off to sneak over when she thought I wasn't looking." Michelle's huff sounded real.

My jaw must've brushed the floor. Why the stealth visit? There was no law against seeing a psychic. "Why didn't I know this?"

"You never asked."

Story of my life. Why couldn't people just spill all the information the first time? Madame Orr's involvement sent my intuition into overdrive. Much as I wanted to march right over and demand answers, I needed more information to have a productive conversation with such a shrewd businesswoman. As in, who was Madame Orr, and exactly how did she fit with Lynda Smythe?

So much for getting a new collar for Gem. I called Sandy before I reached my car. "What do you know about Madame Orr?"

"Good morning to you too," Sandy said.

"Sorry. Hello. How are you this fine morning?"

Sandy's chuckle drew mine. "Never mind. What do you need?"

Was I really that predictable? "Did you know Lynda Smythe was seeing Madame Orr?"

"Seriously?"

"No kidding. Before I talk to her, I need to know everything you can dig up about where she came from. What she did before coming to Barkview. You know the drill."

"You think there's something to this?" Sandy asked.

"Yes," I replied with more confidence than I'd felt in days. "I just dropped Gem at the Fluff and Buff. I'm heading to the Old Barkview Inn to see how the gala's coming together."

"I'm already here. Ty's here, but your aunt needs to send him home. Guy's flushed and feverish."

"So he's not faking?" Maybe his loyalty did extend to Aunt Char and the mayoral office after all.

"No. I really was prepared to hate him over this," Sandy admitted. "The diamonds the GIA included with the Shepard Diamond for the exhibit look magnificent. Glad I bought a new dress. This is a first-class event."

Sandy looked great in a gunny sack. Half the men in Barkview would notice tonight.

While I trusted Sandy's amazing research abilities, Russ's resources could also deliver. I called him about Madame Orr as well.

"Are you telling me that the former mayor's wife was talking to the dead?" Russ asked.

Verbalized, it sounded even more unlikely. "That's the rumor. There's nothing illegal about it."

"It is political suicide. No wonder she kept it quiet."

I hadn't thought about it that way. "So..."

"You figured I'd be a better helper than the chief of police."

No denying my motivation. "Madame Orr is involved. I know it. I just don't know how the pieces fit together yet." There'd be no cooperation from her, either, not without motivation.

"Listen to you." Russ's chuckle drew mine. Maybe I did sound a little like a TV mystery sleuth.

"I'll see what I can find." Russ exhaled. "Nothing more on the Shepard Diamond's history."

"But..."

Russ had something. I heard it in his voice. "I did discover that the Shepard Diamond's loan was approved after the Smithsonian received a significant amber collection from..."

I waited for the drumroll.

"Victor Roma," Russ announced. "He's the chairman of Firebird Industries."

Suddenly a piece fell into place. My heart skipped a beat. "Any relation to our pickleball pros?"

"Victor is their uncle. The twins' father was also a principal until his death in 2015. Firebird Industries is their primary sponsor," Russ explained.

No surprise there. "How did the Romas make their money?"

"Looks like a series of good investments. Beginning, coincidently, right after Victor's grandfather, Victor Senior, emigrated from Romania and applied for political asylum—drumroll—in 1958."

What intriguing timing. "The same year the Shepard Diamond was traded to the Smithsonian."

"Exactly. A year later, both sons married Russian immigrants and purchased two New York apartment buildings."

"With money received from selling the diamonds the Smithsonian traded?"

"Maybe," Russ said. "The boys continued to buy and sell property until 1985, when the sons acquired a construction company that ultimately grew into the Firebird Industries conglomerate we know today."

"Do you think they want the Shepard Diamond back?"

"Victor Roma is a wealthy man. The diamond may have sentimental value."

"The one that got away?" I agreed with Russ's *hmmm*. "It can't be a coincidence that pickleball pros Logan and Loreli are in Barkview at the same time the Shepard Diamond goes missing."

"It is suspect," Russ said.

The injury to Logan's arm suddenly mattered. Talk about an elaborate series of events. Just thinking about all the players and moving parts hurt my head. "Could Victor be pulling the strings?"

"He is an astute businessman," Russ noted.

Certainly smart enough to have an agenda.

"Victor had two daughters. I'm also looking into his brother, Logan and Loreli's father," Russ said.

He'd sort that out. "The big question is, why would Victor Roma care if the Shepard Diamond could be traced to his grandfather?"

"I don't know," Russ said.

Actually, there was more to it than that. "What if Lynda Smythe was right and the Shepard and Douglas Diamonds are related?" I asked.

"That's a leap. The Douglas Diamond disappeared in 1925," Russ reminded me. "Thirty-three years later a previously unknown diamond is donated to the national museum. Isn't it likely the Shepard Diamond is the Douglas Diamond?"

"You're suggesting someone found the Douglas Diamond and, knowing it belonged to the Douglas Trust, traded it to the Smithsonian?" I really hated his logic sometimes. Especially when it made sense.

"You've seen the maps showing that the US military closed Barkview's caves during the 1940s."

"And military personnel did man the coastal warning stations. I suppose someone could've stumbled on the cave

Jonathan Douglas took refuge in." I trusted Russ's judgment. I really did, but...

"Something is telling you otherwise," Russ said.

No concrete evidence. Nothing but a twinge told me to dig deeper into Lynda Smythe's story. "What is your intuition telling you?" I asked.

"To trust yours," he said simply.

My stomach dropped all the way to my toes. He trusted me and my investigative skills. "Why?"

He choked on a chuckle. "Because you are smart and talented and you have proven your hunches are valid."

What wasn't to like about that compliment? I must've beamed.

Russ cleared his throat. "Go back to basics and start digging. The answers are out there."

"I need to get my hands on Lynda's private papers."

"Don't even think about a clandestine visit. Adam Smythe is baiting you into trying something." Russ's skepticism matched my own.

Even I knew that. "The whole thing is a political mine field for me," I added. "I know it seems insane that the Shepard and Douglas Diamonds could be from the same rough. The original stone would have had to have been at least eighty-five carats. But the Russian Revolution ended the Romanov dynasty in 1917. All kinds of jewels went missing."

"The Russians diligently reclaimed their national treasures," Russ stated.

No doubt he'd visited them at the Kremlin, too. "What better way to disguise a significant yellow diamond than recut it into two smaller stones?" I asked. "The stone also could have been given away prior to the revolution."

"A gift for a favored mistress, perhaps?" Russ suggested.

"Nicholas II was reportedly a faithful husband." I'd

Googled that. Except for a ballet dancer prior to his marriage and a fondness for vodka, the late czar had not suffered from the era's usual excesses.

"Royals had secrets," Russ said.

All played out in public today. Back then... "Would have had to have been a significant secret. We are assuming the stone was separated around 1918. What if it happened a generation earlier? I still keep wondering why someone would steal the Shepard Diamond. The Douglas Diamond has been missing for a hundred years." With no new clues where to find it. "Whoever 'they' are must know something about the Douglas Diamond we don't."

"Only one way to find out," Russ said.

"If Logan will even see us." The problem with a society based on law and order was the actual law. Legally, Logan wasn't required to talk to us. I wondered if having won a medal in his pickleball tournament would help. Suddenly, inspiration struck. "Meet me at the Old Barkview Inn. I'm sure Renny wants to go on a playdate."

"No doubt," Russ laughed. "Sounds like a solo act."

"Coward." Had to admire Russ's survival instincts. Renny just might kill me for this.

CHAPTER 12

The Cavalier cold shoulder wasn't exactly murder, but the payback was going to be bigger than a Bichon Bisquets barkery treat. I swear Renny could read my mind. How else could she meet me at the Crown Ballroom door in a huff before I even fully formulated my plan?

I frowned back, my eyes searching for Aunt Char. The Old Barkview Inn's ballroom had been transformed from a simple museum exhibition into a nineteenth-century high-society Victorian celebration. Not so hard to execute in the richly paneled room already decorated with elegant carved pillars and magnificent topiaries. Long windows lined the perimeter, each set in an alcove featuring historical photos depicting Barkview's beginnings in the 1890s. Beneath the crown-shaped chandelier and surrounded by thirty formally-set round tables stood the Shepard Diamond display. Today Max and Maxine stood guard, alongside two armed policemen. Trust Uncle G to perpetuate the diamond myth in style.

I found Ty first, fussing with the blush tea roses in the

floral centerpieces. His light-blue, button-down Oxford shirt and Dockers seemed to swamp his tall, gangly frame.

"'Morning, Cat. Congratulations on your silver medal." Ty's red nose and glassy hazel eyes confirmed Sandy's assessment. The guy wasn't feeling well.

"You should be home in bed," I said.

"Can't leave the mayor in a bind. Nell's chicken soup helped and..." He sneezed so hard he stumbled into a gold-backed Chiavari chair.

I lunged in to help. "Sandy and I are here. We can take care of the last-minute details. You need to take care of yourself."

Ty coughed and winced. "It's my responsibility."

"To not get the rest of us sick." Aunt Char materialized beside us, tapping her loafered foot. "Come back tonight only" —She paused for emphasis—"if you are feeling better."

Ty's half-hearted objection ended in another sneeze that shook him. "I-I'll see you...*ah-choo*."

Ty left without another word. I glanced around the room. Sandy stood at the table assignment board while the catering staff scurried around setting the tables. There was still much to do. Interrogating Logan would have to wait.

Aunt Char patted my arm. "How can I help?"

She said the same words a hundred times a day and meant them. "No. No. What can I do to help you?"

"Find Chris's killer," she ordered.

She didn't need to add, "Find the Shepard Diamond too." Subterfuge bothered her. "Renny looks a little stressed. I think she needs a playdate with Tessa in their suite."

I didn't even look at Renny. Her snort expressed her feelings clear enough. Aunt Char scrolled through her phone and dialed. She smoothly greeted Loreli and begged a favor. "Thank you, my dear. My niece will bring Renny up right now. Yes. So true. All the activity is quite nerve-wracking." Aunt Char hung up. "I'll send bacon-glazed dognuts. Logan can't resist them. Who can?"

Only in Barkview. I'd still take any reason to draw Logan out. Aunt Char handed me Renny's leash. "Be good. Both of you."

Reprimand noted as we huffed in unison. At least Renny walked with me. She didn't heel, exactly, but not needing to drag or carry her had to be a win. "Thank you for doing this," I whispered as Will slid the ornate Otis elevator gates open.

Renny ignored me, instead focusing her big brown eyes on Will. "Miss Renny. Miss Wright, welcome. I will bring your dognuts to the Oxford Suite shortly."

Before I could thank Will, Renny leaned in for a scratch. She sure could take over the show. "So, what's the deal with Logan's injury?" If anyone knew, Will would.

Will sniffed. "Claims he collided with a piece of wood mid-wave."

Really bad luck, but not impossible. "You're not convinced."

"Mr. Logan is a head turner."

No denying that. Add professional athlete to that resume and "irresistible" came to mind. "Anyone in particular?" Maybe Sandy would've been the better investigator here.

"Miss McCarthy," Will replied.

Stephanie McCarthy, the Frosty Pups Creamery owner? Sure, she was cute with pale skin and hair so dark it looked blue-black and perfectly matched her Blue Bay Shepherd's supple coat. "She's..." I didn't know what to say. Since when did the girl-next-door turn a professional athlete's head?

"Not who'd you expect," Will said drily.

No kidding. "So, what really happened?"

Will's shrug hid nothing. He needed a nudge. Boldly, I suggested, "A rendezvous gone wrong?"

His raised-brow surprise was priceless. "I—uh—couldn't say."

But he had. I thanked Will. No need to reconfirm the suite location: Tessa's barking directed me right to the door. Renny ducked behind my legs as the door swung open and a tricolor blur leaped out, colliding with my shins, knocking me backward. I tripped over Renny, my arms flailing, finally connecting with an alcove vase. Disaster... A hand came out of nowhere, clamping on my wrist, saving me from an antique calamity.

Gratefully, I looked into a pair of the most stunning cornflower-blue eyes I'd ever seen. "T-Thank you," I finally managed to say. I noticed the golden highlights shooting through his brown hair and his muscular chest right away.

"No problem." Logan winced as he steadied me. "Tessa the terrorist at work." He massaged his right arm, in a sling close to his waist.

Tessa, a terror? He'd never met Sandy's Jack Russell. That dog would be running circles around all of us while Tessa just sat in Renny's face, panting. No respect for personal space. I owed Renny. She'd never let me forget it either. Better to make it worth it. "You must be Logan. I'm sorry I didn't get to see you play yesterday."

"You won silver in mixed doubles, right?"

"Should've been gold," I muttered not-so-under my breath.

"Ha. We've all said that before. Me included." He pointed to his injured arm. "I'm the real idiot here. Come in." He pointed at Tessa. The dog turned tail and went into the suite. No doubt who was the alpha here.

My foot tap interrupted Renny's quick-exit strategy, and I followed her inside. Like the Windsor, the Oxford Suite had been named after another Barklay Cavalier champion. Decorated in shades of sky blue and cream, this room was furnished in the clean, more modest lines associated with the late Victorian period. Instead of a fireplace, an ornate black-and-silver-accented stove filled the corner near the northwest balcony.

Loreli held Tessa in her arms when we entered. "I am so sorry. Tessa just loves Renny."

"No problem." I ignored Renny's snort. "I ordered some bacon dognuts. They should be up shortly."

"My favorite." Logan, the epitome of trust fund indulgence, lounged on the side chair. "What exactly do dogs do on a playdate?"

Good question. I looked at Loreli. She started to speak, then shut her mouth and said nothing. In desperation, I glanced at Renny, who tossed her head in the do-I-have-to-do-everything way she always got me with. She strolled to Loreli and waited for a head scratch.

"Aw." Loreli fell for it right away and put Tessa down. When she leaned over to scratch both dogs, a gold pendant with a blue evil-eye spilled down her snowy white top. A talisman, or just a gift celebrating her and Logan's brilliant blue eyes? I smiled at Logan. "How long are you laid up for?"

"Hoping just a few weeks."

"If you're lucky. Puncture wounds take time to heal," Loreli added. In Cavalier heaven, she barely noticed me.

My hand went right to my scarf. "Ouch. Impaled by a surfboard." Dog bites caused puncture wounds.

"That would've been a better story. Banged my arm on a two-by-four with rusty nails."

"The tetanus shot bothered him more than the injury," Loreli added. "You did it on purpose so you didn't have to dance with me tonight."

Logan pressed his unbound hand above his heart. "You caught me."

I envied their sibling camaraderie. I'd always wanted a sister. A half-sister twelve years my junior didn't count.

On cue, Will delivered a plate of dognuts and dog treats.

Did I believe them? This pair had their show down, maybe too well. A nail puncture could resemble a dog bite. More than ever, I wished I'd brought Gem to check out Logan, but my playdate excuse never would've worked. Did I dare bring Gem to Aunt Char's event tonight? A German Shepard takedown during cocktails would be worthy of the record book for sure. And it would ruin an otherwise successful Founder's Day.

I glanced at Renny, gnawing on her chew treat beside Tessa. No question they shared a common lineage. Their bone structure and head shape looked similar, as did their attitudes, yet somehow Renny outshone Tessa. Not so different than Loreli and Logan. Although beautiful in her own right, beside her Adonis brother, Loreli paled.

"You both look familiar to me." Strange they endorsed no products or did televised interviews. I'd only seen them on the court during televised matches. Firebird Industries' funding couldn't be that lucrative. Come to think of it, I didn't recall reading any dating gossip about them either.

"Everyone says that." I noted Loreli's sudden unease in the look she shared with her brother.

"People tell me I kinda look like Jennifer Aniston," I said. That analogy fell into the Gen X *huh* pit. Clearly they'd never seen her movies.

Neither sibling commented, making me wonder if one of their relatives had been someone I should know. But according to Russ, they were descendants of Romanian immigrants who possessed a significant yellow diamond. Could they somehow be related to the psychic, Madame Orr, too?

I left with more questions than answers and owing one dogrific-big favor that scared me most of all.

CHAPTER 13

I made it to the Fluff and Buff minutes before Michelle's pick-up-Gem-or-else call. I apologized and double-tipped her. No sense burning that bridge. Lately, emergency grooming appointments popped up as often as my own haircuts. Gem managed to look both fluffy and sleek, with not an airborne hair in sight.

"Don't tell me she needs daily brushes," I grumbled.

"Hourly." Michelle let me panic a long second before smiling.

She was kidding. I think. "Seriously?"

"*Non*. Poor Gem is just stressed." I smelled Michelle's famous lavender biscuits through the paper bag. "Give her one of these and a massage..."

Massage a dog? I'd find Chris's killer first.

Once we were together again, Gem stuck to me like flypaper. I left my car at the salon and stop-and-go tested the dog's heeling skills as we walked the block and a half west on Maple to the Bow Wow Boutique. She didn't miss a beat.

Sporting the same mansard-style roof as most of the

downtown shops, the luxury dog accessories store always brought a stroll down the Champs-Élysées to mind. Misha the fashionista met me at the door. Normally the lead topper on my WDI Scale (that's my Wright Dog Insanity Scale that graded Barkview over-the-topness on a scale of one to fifteen), the long-haired, silky Yorkie dressed in a flowing yellow shirt-dress with a sparkly rhinestone collar didn't even register. When Alicia Bright, dressed in an identical outfit, joined us, I quickly reassessed a WDI matchy-matchy twelve. Twins dressing alike maybe I could get, but owner and dog? Only in Barkview.

"Planning on out-blinging the diamond?" I asked.

Alicia's chocolate-colored eyes glittered with true blingaholic delight. "I'm so excited to see it and the other stones. I've always wanted to visit the Smithsonian."

"You will still need to visit to see the Hope Diamond."

Alicia exhaled dreamily. "Oh, well. Any trip to see jewels is sparklishous."

No argument from me. "I need a new collar for Gem."

Alicia blinked, clearly shocked by the unremarkable stand-in. "What happened to her last one?"

I really should've rehearsed an answer. "Don't ask." Piqued curiosity I could deal with, the truth not so much.

"The workmanship is guaranteed."

She was only trying to help. "Yeah. I'd better buy another one. Please include the tracking feature."

"What tracking feature?" Alicia's confusion couldn't be feigned. Whoever had added the GPS tracker had their own agenda.

"I figured it was something you just added," I said lamely.

"It's a good idea, but most people who want trackers get the J Tracker collar. Most dogs are chipped in case they are lost."

"But that requires a special scanner. Seems to me a tracker would be more proactive. How expensive could it be?" Kids and spouses could be tracked by an app on their phones. Wouldn't Barkviewians want that peace of mind for their BFF?

Alicia didn't respond, which made perfect sense when she rang up the sale. "You can't be serious," I protested. My complaint got me the dreaded raised brow. Who knew an over-the-counter collar could be so expensive? Maybe a J Tracker collar wasn't so overpriced after all. "How many of these things do you sell a year?" It couldn't be many.

"A few a month, including one yesterday to Tessa's mom, Loreli Roma. This is the last one I have until next week, when I get another shipment."

I froze. Sure, I was happy to get the last one, but Loreli's Cavalier wore a pavé diamond J Tracker GPS collar exactly like Renny's. I'd just seen it an hour ago. Why would she buy this jeweled replica? Unless she was trying to conceal something, like the Shepard Diamond, in the scattered multicolored bling.

Alicia tapped her foot. "Do you want the collar?"

As if I had a choice. Alicia disdainfully disposed of the plain collar and adjusted the sparkly one for a perfect fit.

"You look marvelous," Alicia said.

I swear Gem preened. She seemed taller, more regal. "Does Madame Orr come in here with her lamb?" Had to be a lamb. Sheep were bigger.

"A lamb?" Alicia almost choked on her chuckle. "She owns a Bedlington Terrier."

"No way that—that *thing* is a dog. Its head and ears are..."

"It's a dog." Alicia typed on her phone and handed it to me.

If the AKC site hadn't listed the Bedlington Terrier, I'd have sworn the pear-shaped head and tassel ears belonged to a lamb. No wonder the city council hadn't enforced the barn animal ban on her. Still... the dog looked just like a lamb. "Are you sure she's not..."

"Don't say it," Alicia pleaded.

But I had to. "...pulling the wool over your eyes?" It would be just like Madame Orr.

"It really is a dog." The more Alicia read to me about the dog's history, the more I shook my head. A fortuneteller owning a dog revered as a stealth poacher?

"Madame Orr comes in for squeaky toys a few times a week. Apparently, her dog makes a game of separating the squeakers from the toys and hiding them." Alicia squeezed a soft toy for emphasis.

Smart dog. I cringed. The sound got right under my skin. Maybe Gem corralling me wasn't so bad. I bought a squeaky toy just in case. In Barkview, the thoughtful dog toy trumped a 95-point bottle of wine as a hostess gift any day.

Despite my best efforts, I still had more questions than answers. I thanked Alicia and walked another half block west on Maple to the Frosty Pup Creamery. With any luck, Stephanie could tell me what had really caused Logan's injury.

I followed the aroma of freshly baked waffle cones to the restored rumrunners-lookout-turned-beachfront creamery. Outside a shore-rock chimney and paned bay windows paid tribute to the Craftsman-style bungalow's beginnings. Inside, Scandinavian minimalism reigned. Stainless steel yogurt dispensers lined one white subway-tiled wall. The seating area consisted of acrylic block tables with cube chair seating. Glass-mounted dog photos punctuated the white walls.

BB, Stephanie's Blue Bay Shepherd, loped across the black-and-white checkerboard floor to sniff Gem. Butt to nose, the two dogs made a ritual of it. "I guess they know each other," I said.

Dressed in a midnight-blue lab coat, dark pants, and

Skechers, she looked coolly competent and ever-efficient. "BB and Gem attend the same agility training class."

Who'd have guessed? I didn't ask who was better. Mother-bear bias discounted true analysis. Best to get right to business. "Did you see Logan Roma on Wednesday night?"

No words necessary. The two-alarm fire staining her pale checks answered that one. I fished Post-it notes from my pocket and a pen. "Did he hurt his arm surfing?"

Make that a fireball on her face. So much for Logan's tall tale. "What happened?" I asked more gently.

As Stephanie thunked onto a hard plastic chair, BB stepped between us, protecting her, I realized. Not to be outdone, Gem stood between me and BB. Maybe it was a Shepherd thing after all.

Stephanie's hand shook as she stroked BB. Taking a page from Aunt Char's just-listen training, I mentally counted to ten and waited for her to speak. "It wasn't BB's fault. He came in the back door."

"BB bit Logan?" I'd be panicked too, living in zero-biting-tolerance Barkview.

She bobbed her head miserably. "Logan came in for a yogurt on Wednesday afternoon. He'd been running..."

"It was pouring cats and dogs outside." I should know; I'd been soaked through.

"Yeah. He got caught in the downpour. Dripped like a shaggy dog all over my floor."

Not high on neatnik Stephanie's list for sure.

"I tried to mop up, but he wouldn't let me. Insisted on doing it himself."

Lounge-around Logan? That had to be a sight. "You stood there while he mopped the floor?"

Stephanie nodded, starry-eyed. "I'm telling you the truth."

I believed her. I just couldn't picture it. "What happened next?"

"I made him a vanilla and strawberry swirl, and we talked." If possible, her blush deepened. "I'm a sucker for blue eyes, but his… I swear I could see into his soul."

Granted, he did have mesmerizing eyes, but a window onto his soul? I wasn't sure I'd want to look in there, anyway.

"At first I couldn't believe a guy like that would pay attention to me." She cut off my reassurances. "It took me forever to realize it."

I could relate. "It took Sandy and Aunt Char pointing it out to make me realize Russ was interested in me."

"I flirted back," Stephanie admitted.

"You invited him to your place?" I asked.

"Yes. I mean, no, I didn't invite him. He thought I did. It was all a big misunderstanding."

No kidding. "When you refused to let him in your house, he didn't leave?"

"No. I mean, I guess I'd left the side door open."

"And he thought you left the door open for him?" Macho or criminal?

Stephanie nodded. "BB bit him. I swear she was protecting me."

I stilled her panic with a hug. "Logan won't tell anyone." Unless he needed it for an alibi. Smart move. He'd neatly set up Stephanie.

"He swore he wouldn't. He took the blame. Felt really bad about the whole thing. I disinfected the wound and put antibiotic ointment on it, but he couldn't remember the last time he had a tetanus shot, so I took him to the hospital. He made up the story about the nails to avoid questions."

"What time was that?" I asked.

"Around two."

"In the morning?" The timing cleared Logan of nothing, and it begged the question, what had he been doing up until then?

Stephanie nodded. "Please, Cat. BB isn't a biter. She was only protecting me."

I made a note and patted Stephanie's hand. "I won't tell anyone. One more thing. Was there anything unusual about the bite?"

"What do you mean?" she asked.

"Was the shape odd?"

She shrugged. "I'm no expert, but it seemed deeper than I thought it would be."

"Why?"

"BB wasn't trying to hurt him, just scare him, but the wound was deep. Made me realize how strong her jaw is."

I swallowed hard, my scarf constricting. That I could relate to.

"There's something I meant to talk to you about." Stephanie had my attention. "We"—Her gesture included both BB and Gem—"practice at the agility course adjacent to the train station. Monday afternoon, I saw Chris Papas there. He met with a man in an old Bark U hoodie."

My pulse jumped. Was this the lead I'd been waiting for? "Did Chris bring Gem to practice often?"

"Sometimes. This meeting was odd. Chris kept looking over his shoulder while he was walking over there," Stephanie explained.

I made another note. "What did the guy in the sweatshirt look like?"

"Kinda tall. Towered over Chris."

Next to the compact gymnast, everyone seemed gigantic. "What do you mean by an old hoodie?"

"It was the vintage logo." She must've read my blank look. "You know, the fifty-year-anniversary version of the logo."

Right. That made the hoodie at least three years old and eliminated Logan Roma. I pulled up Chad Williams's *Finders Keepers Treasure* website on my phone. It was a long shot, but the archaeologist had been hunting for the Douglas Diamond for some time. "Is this him?"

Stephanie's brows knitted. "I don't know. Maybe. The whole incident totally weirded me out."

Not exactly an identification that would convince a prosecutor, but worth a visit. I shared my yogurt with Gem on our walk back to my car. Was it a coincidence that Logan had been bitten by a dog on the same arm as one of Ariana's attackers? Not likely.

Did I dare give Gem a shot at him? A dog's testimony might count in Barkview, but not in California criminal court. BB's bite neatly explained Logan's injury. Without other proof, Logan would get away with the murder of Chris Papas.

If accusations started flying, no telling how long Logan would stay in town either. If he had been sent by his uncle, would he continue searching for the Shepard Diamond or cut his losses? What role did Madame Orr and Lynda play? And how did the Douglas Diamond fit in?

CHAPTER 14

With more questions than answers, I drove east on Cottonwood past the Barkview Hospital and up the bluffs to Bark U, Barkview's nationally acclaimed university. Maybe Chad Williams, *Finders Keepers Treasures* blogger and self-proclaimed diamond expert, could tell me something new about the Douglas Diamond's origins.

I found the youthful Leonardo DiCaprio look-alike dressed in the Bark U sweatshirt Stephanie had described and tight jeans in his university office. A teacher's assistant for the dean of the Science Department, Chad's book-lined office brought to mind a walk-in-closet with a lagoon view. Low clouds hung off the coast, poised to cloak the beach in winter's chill. I made a note to bring a warm wrap to tonight's event.

Gem announced our arrival before I could with a deep, intimidating *grrrr* and sat at my feet.

Chad's pretty-boy-adventurer demeanor disappeared as he cowered behind his paper-piled steel desk, shouting, "Keep that dog away from me."

As if a few books and tests could protect him from Gem.

Reminiscent of my last visit with Sandy and her Jack Russell when investigating Jan Douglas's death, I had to wonder what secrets Chad had to draw the same response from both dogs. "Relax. She only attacks on command."

His sidelong glance almost made me burst out laughing. Me, order a dog attack? The universe did have a sense of humor. "As long as you had nothing to do with Chris Papas's murder, you'll be fine."

His swivel chair protested as he plopped down. "The jewelry store owner I read about this morning?" His eye strayed to the newspaper scattered across his leather side chair.

Not an auspicious beginning. I still readied a Post-it and snatched a pen from the cup on his desktop.

"Tell me what you discussed with Chris Papas on Monday at the train station."

"I didn't meet him on Monday." His confusion seemed real enough, but his darting eyes said there was more.

"My mistake. When did you meet him?"

"Maybe a month ago."

So Chris wasn't just some random guy in the newspaper as Chad had originally stated. "What did you talk about?"

"I asked him if two diamonds could be reconnected."

How did Chad know about the possible link between the Douglas and Shepard Diamonds? "What did he say?" I asked.

"Not likely after separate cutting and polishing. It might be possible to confirm if they came from the same rough," he explained.

No subterfuge. I believed him. "For the record, where were you Monday evening between five and seven?"

Chad checked his calendar. "In the Special Collections Library until 11 p.m."

I made a note on my Post-it. "Can anyone verify that?"

His “duh” reminded me a university library had all kinds of witnesses.

“I didn’t kill Chris Papas. I hardly knew him.”

That I believed. “Why did you ask about connecting the diamonds?”

He chewed his lip. I persisted. “Who told you the Shepard and Douglas Diamonds were once connected?” Might as well lay it all out.

It worked. Chad basketed his head in his hands, deflated. “How did you find out?”

“I know everything.” Not really. Sandy and Russ did. I just asked the questions.

My boast still got right under his skin. Chad squirmed before answering. “Jonathan Douglas spoke to me.”

I couldn’t have heard him right. “The rumrunner who’s been missing for a hundred years?”

“Yeah.” No hiding his wariness. I’d be defensive too. “Madame Orr said...”

Not the psychic again. My jaw clenched. I couldn’t help myself.

Chad misread my disdain. “The diamond will be found this year.” His dead-dog seriousness just begged an argument.

No point giving in. Twenty painful seconds ticked by. Gem growled. Bicuspids bared, the dog intimidated well. Truthfully, I enjoyed Chad’s big-eyed dive for cover. There was something to be said about an intimidating protector. “Your poker face needs work,” I remarked.

Chad’s cheeks colored. “It’s my find.”

No sense debating that point either. “The diamond has been lost for four generations. What makes you think you can find it now?” Without a fresh clue, he couldn’t with any certainty.

"Under a waning moon, the diamond will be reunited in the hundred-and-twentieth year."

My nape hairs tingled. "A prophecy? You can't be serious."

The cat-ate-the-canary look in his dark eyes indicated otherwise. Forget science and countless research hours. "Even if it's true, you still have twenty-three years to wait," I added.

Lottery-fever brightened in his dark eyes. "The diamond was lost a hundred years ago. It was separated from its soul long before then."

Too many questions cluttered my mind. First, how could he possibly know all this, and second, no doubt, a diamond said "buy me" on a regular basis. But how could it have a soul? "What are you uniting the Douglas Diamond with exactly?"

"Its other half." No hesitation. He believed.

"I see. Adam Smythe claims the same thing. How did you verify his claim?" I'd love to get my hands on that information.

"No. Not Adam Smythe. Madame Orr said..."

Without Gem's furry shoulder braced against me, I'd have done a face-plant. Like it or not, the crooked path led directly to the fortuneteller. "When research fails, your go-to answer is a fortuneteller." The hypothesis sounded even more absurd verbalized.

"Why not? I had nothing to lose," Chad insisted, only slightly sheepishly.

"Except your reputation." Gem nudged at my side. She sensed it too. "Madame Orr saw this in her very own crystal ball? She saw your 'soulmate' too. Didn't she?"

A three-alarm fire burned on his cheeks. The woman was a bona fide charlatan. No arguing with a true believer. "Tell me how she knows that this year is the hundred-twentieth year referred to in the prophecy?"

"The spirit told her."

Shocked that an intelligent academic had fallen for this fantasy, I could only ask, "What spirit?"

No response. I tapped my foot.

Chad buckled under my scrutiny. "A woman. She never said who she was exactly."

Of course not. Fortunetelling relied on innuendo and ambiguity. The big question was, why would Madame Orr lead Chad down this path? What did she need from him? Where did her information originate? What part did Lynda Smythe play?

"She seemed so sure." He balanced his head in his hands, his forehead hooded beneath the Bark U sweatshirt. Had he finally seen his folly?

"She can be convincing..." I said lamely.

"I'm an idiot." He repeated that again and again.

No argument from me. "What information did she want from you?"

He perked up. "N-nothing."

I crushed his hope. "What stuff did you chat about?"

"She's a closet geologist. Really well read in stratigraphy."

I scribbled the phonetic spelling but had to confirm. "Strati-what?"

"Stratigraphy. The study of rock layers, the strata, and layering, stratification. It's..."

I stuffed a Posit-it in my pocket and glanced at my bold Google watch. Never ask a teacher for an explanation when faced with a time crunch. I tuned out the rest, waiting for a chance to interrupt. "So, she wanted to know about the caves you explored with Jan Douglas?"

Jan Douglas had been Jonathan Douglas's last living direct descendant and a fevered hunter of the Douglas Diamond. I'd met Chad and Sandy eighteen months ago when Jan had been murdered for reasons unrelated to the diamond.

He stopped mid-sentence, his open jaw an invitation to flying pests. "Y-yes."

No need to say more. He got it. Madame Orr was after "his" treasure. But was the information in her prophecy real or just fabricated to gain Chad's trust?

"For the sake of argument, let's say the Douglas Diamond is part of a pair. What diamond is its match?"

"I don't know for sure, but it has to be the Shepard Diamond. It's the only color match that would be about the right size."

"And you intend to steal the Shepard Diamond for confirmation." Antsy Chad couldn't sit in silence for any time, never mind outlast me.

His confusion seemed real enough. "Steal it? Why? I'd apply for an academic viewing exception."

A good option. Nervous Nelly Chad craved social acceptance and fame. Secretly solving a mystery wouldn't meet his needs. "You've clearly thought about this. Did you find anything out about the original diamond? It had to be eighty carats. Where did it come from?" I asked. "A diamond that size doesn't just materialize out of nowhere."

Chad folded his hands into lecture mode. "The Royal Mining Academy of Berlin controlled the Pomona mine in Southern Namibia from 1886 to 1915. Those alluvial mines ultimately produced over a million carats with little oversight."

"An eighty-carat fancy yellow diamond still would've been reported. Look at the pomp and ceremony the Cullinan Diamond received." My diamond knowledge really was coming in handy.

"True. During the Victorian and Edwardian eras, European aristocracy accumulated jewels." Chad scratched his forehead. "What if this stone was intended to be a bridal gift?"

"For a German princess?" I asked.

"The most famous German princess about that time was Alix of Hesse."

"The empress of Russia," I said. The Russian angle kept coming up too.

"And Queen Victoria's favorite granddaughter. Since we know the Douglas Diamond was purchased in London, it makes sense that a British aristocrat acquired the original yellow stone, likely from a German source."

"Britain and Germany were at war." World War I changed the world.

"That started in 1914. It was said Queen Victoria's offspring sat on every European throne at the turn of the nineteenth century," Chad explained. "King George, Kaiser Wilhelm, and Czar Nicholas were first cousins. It's been said that World War I would never have happened if Victoria had been alive."

I exhaled. Lots of possibilities with no tangible proof. I thanked Chad for his information and left in a puff of German Shepherd hair despite the triple washing and brushing Gem had undergone earlier that day.

I dialed Sandy en route to my car. "Hey. No need to come back. We have this covered," she announced.

Guilt struck. I'd neatly dodged all the prep work. "I owe you one."

"Only one?"

Good point. "Sorry to bug you, but all roads are leading to Madame Orr. Any info I should know about?"

"Just the usual stuff. Her business license was granted five years and six days ago to Anna Orr. She's a widow. No children. Last address was in Sedona, Arizona, the vortex center of North America. Her website says she's a psychic."

"Where did her money come from?" No way had she generated enough revenue telling fortunes to live the beach lifestyle she enjoyed in Barkview.

"Looks like a life insurance policy paid out when her husband passed. She owns the property her studio or office or whatever she calls it sits on. I'll keep digging. Do you want me to make you an appointment?"

I checked the time. I should call it a day right now and go home to change for tonight's event. "No. If she's really a psychic, she'll know I'm coming." I motioned Gem to jump into my passenger seat.

"It doesn't work like that," Sandy said.

"Like what? She's supposed to predict the future."

"Not exactly. She connects with people you've lost to guide your future. It's more a here-and-now thing."

"You've been to one?"

"Yeah. It's a pretty common party thing. I admit that it was creepy. The lady I visited knew some stuff I'd never told anyone."

"About what? Generalities can be applied to just about any situation. A good judge of character can easily latch onto your emotions," I said.

"It was unnerving, really... never mind. I take it you've been to one too."

"Not me. My mother went after my dad died." My bitterness must have been plain in my voice.

"What happened?"

"Same old stuff any grieving widow wants to hear. The psychic said my dad was sorry to leave her and wanted her to go on with her life, blah, blah, blah."

"Did it help your mom?" asked Sandy.

"If remarrying in six months was the goal, then I guess so." The pain hadn't lessened any over the years.

“And now I know why you never talk about your family,” Sandy said.

What else could she really say?

“Do you want me to talk to Madame Orr?” she asked.

“No. I’m fine.”

I expected an argument. After a moment’s pause, she said, “I’m sure you are. Just try not to kill the messenger.”

CHAPTER 15

Sandy's words resonated as I parked in front of the yellow-and-white-gabled Victorian. I swear the curtain above the daffodils and early tulips peeking through variegated coleus swished as Gem paused at the stone walkway, sniffing, I wish I knew what. To know who had been here before me would be helpful. I needed to shake off my predisposition fast or risk tipping off the arguably all-knowing woman.

I nudged Gem through the bright yellow door. We paused mid-step in the doorway. The whole experience surprised me. From my mother's stories, I'd expected a venue out of the Arabian Knights, with colorful wall hangings and apotropaic symbols. The rich Agarwood scent coupled with the gray-and-navy wallpaper and the polished wood floors brought a chic parlor to mind. A round, café-sized wood table separated two comfy wing-back chairs upholstered in beige. No crystal ball in sight, but that deck of oversize celestial tarot cards on the tabletop might as well have been neon.

I gritted my teeth. A card reading. Gem sensed my anxiety

right away. She positioned herself between me and Madame Orr, advancing only as I did, her stance ready-to-defend. Oddly, the dog's presence calmed me. Whatever happened next, I knew she'd defend me to the end. Come to think of it, I'd been sleeping better than I ever had with her on guard. *Hmmm.*

I focused on Madame Orr. Dressed in a shimmering, flowing robe, the large-boned woman seemed to float across the area rug. "Welcome, Catalina."

I inclined my head, avoiding her heavily charcoaled, dark-as-night eyes. There was something unsettling about the contrast her plaited black hair and pale skin created alongside that white I-can't-believe-it's-not-a-lamb dog at her feet. Even Gem took a second look.

"You have something for Danior?" It didn't take a mind reader to figure out who the Bow Wow Boutique bag belonged to.

I removed the fluffy white sheep from the bag. With a quick head shake, the odd dog took the toy from my hand. Three squeaks later, both paws held the toy to the floor while his teeth dug into the fur.

"Thank you. Danior enjoys the hunt," Madame Orr said.

More like disembowelment. That toy wouldn't last the hour.

"You have questions for me?" Her singsong voice gave me the creeps.

"I expect you know."

"Contrary to popular belief, I am not a mind reader, nor can I predict the future. Though knowing the winning lottery numbers would be helpful." Her smile seemed genuine as she motioned for me to sit at the table. "I will show you what I do know."

Gem blocked the offered chair until she had thoroughly

sniffed the area. I waited until she tossed her head and stepped aside. Madame Orr's perceptive gaze never wavered. She allowed me to be seated before taking her own, in what seemed like an ever-so-slightly more elevated chair. No doubt designed to intimidate. She shuffled the blue and gold cards and laid the first five on the tabletop.

I added card shark to her list of talents when the first card revealed a dog.

"Ah. The moon card." Her lilting voice drew me in, despite my determination to resist.

"The moon's light can bring you clarity and understanding, and you should allow your intuition to guide you through this darkness. I see a great journey." Her gaze held mine.

About as vague as expected. I frowned, stoically giving away nothing.

"Be patient. You will find your soulmate," Madame Orr continued.

Of course I would. Didn't every thirty-something woman want to hear that? Tell them what they want to hear. That's how fortune-telling worked. I started to speak, but a sudden chill blasted through me. Madame Orr started. "Kit Cat?" Gone was the soft, lulling voice, replaced by directness.

I froze. No one called me that anymore.

"A-a man. He was close to you." Again, those eyes bored into me. "Your father?"

She couldn't possibly know. It was his name for me. I'd never told anyone. Not even Aunt Char.

"He wants you to go to Loompaland."

A tidal wave of memories crashed over me. For a split second, I wanted to believe I could communicate with my dad. I could ask him for advice and see his loving smile.

Madame Orr's calculating dark eyes snapped me out of it.

Dad must've told someone about our happy place in chocolate heaven.

"You can't know the truth," Madame Orr continued.

But I would. I'd sworn the day I dumped my Kit Kat stash into Sharks Cove that classified or not, someday I would know how my father died. Enough toying with my emotions. I yoga-breathed. "I'd like to know who told you to tell Lynda Smythe and Chad Williams that the Shepard and Douglas Diamonds were cut from the same stone."

Except for a long blink, Madame Orr showed no reaction. "Who is not important."

"Oh, but it is. If you can conjure up my father, surely you can discern who is speaking to you about the diamonds." Later I'd figure out how she'd ferreted out the info on my dad. Right now I needed more pressing answers.

Her brow raise acknowledged that truth. I waited. She just stared at me. So much for Aunt Char's silence technique.

"I'm guessing the original stone was roughly eighty carats." I shaped my thumb and forefinger into a circle the size of a robin's egg. "This big. No wonder it had a soul. That kind of majesty belonged to a monarch back in the nineteenth century, and even then only a handful could've acquired it." The more I thought about it, there had to be a record of an eighty-carat African yellow diamond. Something that size couldn't be kept secret.

Madame Orr's battle for nonchalance played in her jawline. I'd gotten close, too close, it seemed. Her tight words proved it. "I tell what I see. I am not privy to a spirit's life story."

"But you do know something about this one." I couldn't bring myself to call it a spirit. A historical figure made so much more sense, but who was it?

"Not always."

This "spirit" certainly had a name and Madame Orr knew or knew of it. I could tell. Time to push her a little. "Let me help with a few, uh, known facts. In 1920, a British diamond broker sold a yellow diamond fit for a "queen" to a rich American. This stone was subsequently lost. In 1958, a man from Romania traded the supposed other half of this mega-gem to the Smithsonian." Madam Orr relaxed ever so slightly. If I hadn't been watching her so closely, I'd have missed it. I had something wrong. Did the Russian angle mean something?

"Not a Romanian. A Russian noble who'd escaped the Bolsheviks." Who else could have acquired an eighty-carat stone and have it cut with no one the wiser? In 1900, no excess was too much for Russian royalty. In fact, czarist Russia made Louis XVI's Versailles seem minimalist.

No tangible response from Madame Orr. Clearly, losing control of the narrative didn't work for her. "You must have something to add," I said. "An eighty-carat yellow diamond with a prophecy is a stone for a czar."

Her dark eyes flashed just before Gem let out a protective growl. Instinctively, I ducked behind the German Shepherd, glad for the protection. If looks could kill, I'd have been flayed on the spot. No doubt I'd guessed at least a part of the Shepard and Douglas Diamonds' secret, but why did it matter, more than a century later? The Smithsonian legally owned the Shepard Diamond. The Douglas Diamond remained lost and, if ever found, was the property of the Douglas Trust.

I did wonder if the Smithsonian had known the stone's origins. If so, it could be an embarrassment. Two eighteen-carat yellow diamonds, even if someone could prove custody, were pretty, but wouldn't have much effect on world events.

Maybe the bigger question was Madame Orr's part. Was she in some way related to Firebird Industries and Logan

Roma? How did Lynda Smythe fit into all this? Ugh. My head spun with unanswered questions.

I took a deep breath, suddenly looking forward to the black-tie event with Russ. Not only did I value his opinion, but the man loved a good puzzle as much as I did.

CHAPTER 16

I took Gem on her evening walk, still contemplating the wisdom of bringing the dog to the gala. Since the outcome of the event reflected on Aunt Char's leadership, Gem possibly taking down Logan would not be viewed favorably. There had to be another way to arrange a meeting between Gem and Logan.

The sinking sun hung on the horizon, allowing only long strands of orange light to peek through the low coastal clouds as Gem sniffed every post along the boardwalk. I kept glancing at the minute hand on my watch as the standard quarter-of-a-mile walk extended farther and farther. The moment we reached the park's grassy area, Gem nudged me toward her favorite palm tree, circled, and promptly squatted. I remembered the pooper-scooper I'd left in my trunk even before the first drop.

And it kept coming until the pile turned into a heap, and a steaming one at that. Visions of the last disintegrating poop bag I'd used flashed through my mind. I looked warily around. Did I dare to abandon the load and return with that pooper-scooper device? Call me paranoid, but I felt too many prying eyes focused on me. No doubt posting this potential fiasco on social media. No other options available, I yanked two bags from the leash holder, quickly added another just to be sure, and triple-covered my hand. No reason to take a chance any bag was defective, despite Russ's assurance that he'd confirmed otherwise.

Resigned, I waited until Gem circled the mound for the umpteenth time and sat to one side of it. I sucked in my breath and reached... The instant warmth didn't bother me anywhere near as much this time. The lumpiness did. What in the world had Gem eaten?

Clarity struck. Instinctively, I pressed the mush downward and felt a grape-sized rock. OMG! Had I just found the elusive Shepard Diamond? No wonder it had been missing. Gem had swallowed it. And not by chance, either. That dog only ate on command. I suddenly got why Ariana insisted I patrol Gem's poop. She or Chris had instructed the dog to swallow the diamond, which was no bigger than a standard dog treat. Talk about a safe hiding place.

No longer grossed-out, I quickly tied the bag and hot-footed it home, trying hard to act casual while my heart pounded. I bolted my door and flip-closed the shutters before regloving my hands and digging the oval sphere out of the poop bag. I ignored the smelly mush and placed the oval-shaped prize into the sink. A few water splashes later, deep yellow flashes glowed through the brown muck.

I sucked in my breath as I finished spraying off the stone. Up close, its inner light drew me deep into the prisms, offering a teasing glimpse of so much. If the Douglas Diamond completed the circle... I suddenly understood what the two stones together represented and why someone would kill for them. The fire promised so much more than beauty. I saw dynastic riches and the power to shape history, peppered with responsibility, the oppressive kind that could easily break the bearer.

I shook my head and covered the stone with a leopard-print towel, breaking the spell. I breathed hard as I considered my options. If I returned the diamond to the authorities now, Aunt Char's career would be safe and catching Chris's killer became someone else's responsibility. Ariana's words haunted me: "*You will do what needs to be done.*"

Had she chosen me because on occasion I did color outside the lines? Breaking into Howard Looc's casino hotel room hadn't been exactly legal, but it had proven invaluable to finding his killer. The problem now was that I didn't think returning the Shepard Diamond was the right thing to do. We had no idea who had murdered Chris or had orchestrated this elaborate scheme to steal the diamond. We also didn't know who leaked the diamond's inscription codes from either the Smithsonian or the GIA. Would returning it now give the thieves another chance to steal it?

No easy answers here. Responsibility pressed down hard on me. Silence opened me to a federal obstruction charge. While I trusted Uncle G, Aunt Char, and Russ to do the right thing, legalities limited their choices. I took a deep breath. I really had no choice at all.

I stashed the Shepard Diamond in the safest place I could think of, buried beneath a struggling cactus Sandy had given me when I'd proven I could even kill a succulent. My quandary about bringing Gem to the gala resolved itself. I trusted no one more to protect the diamond. The dog seemed to understand and positioned herself between the door and the terra-cotta pot.

With time running out before Russ arrived, I sprinted to my bedroom. I stepped into my three-quarter-length rhinestone-accented black sheath dress and quickly applied shimmer shadow and extra lash-lengthening mascara. A couple of messy curls later, I turned off my curling iron just as Russ rang the doorbell. At least I figured it was Russ from Gem's single happy bark. How I figured that out kind of messed with my head, too.

If anyone tells you a man dressed in a tuxedo and carrying a dozen long-stemmed red roses isn't a fantasy come true, they are either lying or jealous. My knees went weak as he kissed me, his all-male cologne tickling my senses. "You look like a million dollars."

"Not quite that much." I sure felt like it, though, under his hot gaze. "Will you clasp my necklace?"

Russ's fingers brushed my nape as he fastened the Barklay anniversary necklace, on loan from Aunt Char, around my neck. The magnificent five-carat teardrop white diamond sat perfectly on my décolletage.

I leaned in for a kiss. Gem's furry head popped between us. Really?

Russ blinked, the moment gone. He stepped back and shaded his eyes. "You'll blind the crowd with that one."

I laughed. I'd asked to borrow this piece the moment the gala's Diamonds Are Forever theme had been announced. I did feel special in the piece. Russ's sneeze wrecked the moment. So much for Gem's bath alleviating his allergies.

I placed the roses in a crystal vase and grabbed my lacy shawl, knowing full well that Russ's jacket would replace the wispy fabric soon enough. I noted a clump of fluffy Shepherd hair on his shoulder. The black fabric attracted the silken tuffs like a magnet. He needed to get away from Gem or risk having red eyes all night long.

I motioned to him that I was ready to go.

“Gem’s not coming?” No censure in Russ’s tone, just surprise. He knew I took my dog-sitting duties seriously.

“No. I refuse to ruin Aunt Char’s event with unprosecutable actions.” Despite practicing my response, it still sounded wooden to my ears. Keeping anything from Russ didn’t sit well at all and was fraught with danger. The man read me like a favorite book.

Russ eyed Gem, who after interrupting us had returned to her guard position between the planter and the door. “Your aunt’s priority is justice for Chris and finding the diamond.”

Did his voice linger on the word “diamond”? He couldn’t possibly know I had it, but I still felt guilty. “I-I know.” Was it foolish to keep the diamond’s location secret? I’d taken that responsibility on alone, without counsel, to protect him, Aunt Char, and Uncle G. Responsibility chafed. “I met Madame Orr today.” I swallowed hard.

“We are late. You can tell me about it on the way.” Russ led me into the foggy evening air to his Land Rover, the feel of his hand at the small of my back sending a delicious tingle to my toes.

En route I filled him in on my visits with both Chad and Madame Orr.

“If you think the Russian angle needs to be explored, I’ll see what Blue Diamond can piece together,” Russ said.

No argument. His faith in me felt good. The valet opened my car door before I could thank him. We entered the Old Barkview Inn and followed in the footsteps of the first Founder’s Day guests down the plush red carpet through the polished wood lobby to the elegant Crown Ballroom, where the smell of tea roses replaced beeswax. Ty, dressed in a high-necked Victorian waistcoat that fit him more like a corset than a vest, greeted us from behind the check-in table. Although still pale, he looked markedly better than earlier.

He sniffled as he handed me our program and table assignment card. “I’m feeling better since I started taking antibiotics for a sinus infection. I… ah-choo.”

Much as I appreciated his commitment to Aunt Char, the violent sneeze sent a tremor all the way to his feet. “Ty, go home. I’ll take over.” I’d have preferred to mingle with the other guests and watch the Shepard Diamond personally, but even non-germaphobes would find Ty’s constant sneezing unnerving.

“No. It’s my responsibility…” He sneezed again.

Aunt Char breezed by in a midnight dress with a glittering sash inspired by the Milky Way. Pear-shaped diamond earrings sparkled on her ears, competing with the Celeste Barklay pavé diamond choker that matched Renny's collar. While Aunt Char stood purposefully, Renny preened in her champion Cavalier way that made me shake my head every time.

“Enough, young man. Time for you to go home and rest,” Aunt Char insisted.

Renny ended further objections with a majestic toss of her head. Ty sneezed again. “I can’t fight the three of you.”

I slid right into the chair he’d vacated. “You did most of the work. There are only a few stragglers.” Three, to be exact. “I won’t be long.”

“I’ll check on security.” Russ acknowledged my comment with a nod and disappeared into the ballroom. High-tech motion and heat sensors would be focused on the Shepard Diamond at all times tonight, except during the Founder’s Day celebration display. If the thieves intended to attempt to steal the diamond again, that would be the best window of opportunity.

Aunt Char and I watched Ty exit through the front door. “Go inside. I’m fine here,” I said.

Aunt Char didn't budge. "You are glowing, my dear," she announced. "What have you discovered?"

Was I really that transparent? "Nothing I can do anything about now." Which was true. "Go back inside and enjoy your event. You've earned it."

I could see the strain in Aunt Char's half-smile. "'Enjoy' might be a reach today, wondering if the Shepard Diamond will be snatched next." A waiter in Victorian attire approached Aunt Char and requested assistance. She nodded in my direction and followed him toward the lulling string quartet seated by the dais.

Stuck, I crinkled my neck, straining to see past the rose topiaries. No such luck. I removed my phone from my beaded black evening bag and texted Sandy to keep an eye on Adam Smythe. This would be the optimal time to embarrass Aunt Char. Until I figured out his role, he remained on my watch-closely list. I quickly assessed the remaining table assignment cards. Gabby's tardiness didn't really surprise me. The woman would be late for her own wedding.

Murmuring voices and laughter drew my attention inside. I checked the time. Fifteen minutes until dinner service. I'd give the stragglers ten more minutes before joining the festivities.

Gabby sprinted up to me moments before my planned departure, dressed in a beaded, calf-length black dress and impossibly high heels, with her hair swept in an elegant chignon. I hardly recognized the messy-ponytailed barista.

Breathing hard, she apologized. "So sorry. I couldn't get away today. I'm crazy busy."

No empathy from me. "Quit driving your help away," I suggested.

Arms crossed, she huffed. "Easy for you to say. There's only one Sandy."

True. I knew my good fortune. I didn't remind her that

Sandy and I had endured murder to get where we were today. Literally.

"I'm surprised you're still manning this table. I figured I was on my own when I saw Ty in the parking lot arguing with Chelsea."

"Chelsea Smythe?" The former mayor was up to something. I just knew it. Why else would his daughter be arguing with my aunt's assistant? Ty should've been long gone by now. Had this meeting been prearranged, or did it happen by chance? Who was I kidding? Coincidence didn't happen around Chelsea.

"Yes. They weren't really arguing. Ty didn't say a word. Chelsea was beating him up good, though," Gabby explained. "She sure inherited her mother's sharp tongue. I felt sorry for Ty. He had his tail between his legs."

Only in Barkview could a six-foot-something guy be described that way. "What was Chelsea mad about?"

Gabby shrugged. "Wish I knew."

I bet she did. Talk about fresh gossip for the morning Daily Wag crowd.

"Chelsea clammed up and just inclined her head to me when I walked by," Gabby continued.

What I wouldn't give to know the root of that argument. I directed Gabby inside the ballroom. Since Chelsea hadn't passed by me yet, I figured she'd still be outside.

Abandoning the check-in desk, I slipped out the front door in time to see the taillights of Ty's white Prius fade into the mist. I hugged my arms to my chest as I peered through the fog in search of Chelsea. Not even a shadow shifted in the pitch-black darkness. Except for the sound of what could only be faint heel-clicks on the concrete walkway, I'd swear I was all alone. I followed the tip-tapping around the building until the surf drowned out even that sound.

No clue where to go next, I reentered the Old Barkview Inn through a side alcove French door off the lobby and just about tripped over Gabby lurking like a B-movie spy behind a rose topiary. "Who is that woman?" She pointed to a black-caped figure standing at the entrance to a corded-off hallway.

No missing Angela Cooper's artistic silver hair comb, even in the soft lighting. "She's the security director from the GIA."

"The Gemological Institute? Really? Why would she meet with Madame Orr at Barklay Park?"

Gabby got me with that one. I blinked. "Are you sure?"

"Absolutely. It was Tuesday evening, right before the after-dinner rush," Gabby replied. "They both tried to hide behind their umbrellas, but you know I never forget a face."

Gabby's epic recall made me a believer. Why would the GIA director be meeting with Barkview's local psychic? Even more interesting, why was the same GIA representative skulking down a corded-off hallway that ran parallel to the Crown Ballroom?

I followed, not at all certain I trusted the fevered glitter in Gossip Gabby's dark eyes. Keeping secrets wasn't exactly Gabby's forte. Fortunately, Angela led us right to the ladies lounge.

Gabby and I shared a laugh over our paranoia until a strawberry-blonde woman dressed in a black designer coat-dress ensemble and a stunning diamond-and-ruby necklace exited with Angela. A small, reddish dog head with feathered Papillon ears peeked out of a beaded carry bag.

"Whoa. Ruby and Jacob Samuels at the same party after their nasty divorce?" Must be serious gossip fodder, the way renewed excitement lit Gabby's expression.

"Ruby is Isaac Samuels's ex-sister-in-law?" Odd that the GIA's security director appeared more chummy with an ex than the Samuels and Sons owners.

I slipped a Post-it from my beaded purse. Of course I'd brought a pad with me. Doesn't everyone stuff Post-its into a beaded lipstick-tissue-and-phone-sized evening bag? My pen search came up with nothing, though. Great. I committed the need to look deeper into Angela to memory. "How do you know Ruby? She's not a Barkview resident."

"She's an amaretto cappuccino junkie. Came in on Tuesday and again on Thursday just before closing. Took a Meister Blizzard to go on Thursday, too."

Gabby's Jägermeister and coffee with whipped cream hadn't been as popular as she'd hoped. I couldn't hide my cringe. "Are you really selling any of that abomination?"

Gabby's short list of followers included Ty. Now, there was a guy who should be banned from caffeine. "Anything else about her?" I asked.

"Seemed nice enough. Her Russkiy is adorable. She never goes anywhere without it. I think it's a comfort dog. Rumor has it she has a temper."

Another dog breed I'd never heard of. Who could possibly keep up with 195 recognized dog breeds plus 70 wannabes? I can't even think about the infinite mix options either. I didn't ask. I'd see the dog soon enough. "Don't all redheads have a temper? That comfort-dog thing allows you to take your dog everywhere."

"So? You can take your dog everywhere."

"In Barkview. There is a whole wide world out there." In which Ruby traveled extensively.

"Exactly why I never leave town," Gabby admitted.

"You left your dog at home tonight," I pointed out.

"Much to his annoyance. I had the choice to bring him. That's what I'm talking about."

No argument from me. I supported freedom of choice.

"Bet you didn't know Ruby facilitated the Shepard

Diamond coming to Barkview. She consults with Sotheby's now. Wonder if she's here to help or hurt her ex," Gabby added.

Interesting. Records showed Jacob had orchestrated the diamond's loan. "Would she help him?"

"Can't imagine why, after the way Jacob treated her. Can you believe he told her that her dog's pedigree was better than hers?"

"She told you that?" I had to admire Gabby's ability to get people to talk.

"Not in so many words. Samuels and Sons hasn't been doing so well since she left. That would seriously make my day. Jacob Samuels had an in-your-face affair. Serves him right that a stray bit him on his Friday-morning run."

I did a double take. Two dog bites in Barkview in the same week couldn't be a coincidence. "Where was he bit?"

"His left arm is in a sling. They didn't catch the dog, so he needed a tetanus shot." Gabby's half-smile was evil.

Could Ariana in her stupor have confused which of her intruder's arms Gem had bitten? "What kind of dog was it?" I asked.

"Jacob called it a mongrel, but it sounded like a Pit Bull mix of some sort."

I cringed. Couldn't help it. Much as I tried to forget my Pit Bull attack, some things just triggered the memory. I did shake it off quickly. "Ruby told you all that?"

"The EMT told me about the dog. Ruby warned me to stay clear of Jacob. The rest I Googled," Gabby said.

Conclusion by innuendo could only be hearsay. "Ruby has a vested interest in Samuels and Sons succeeding. She owns twenty percent of the business."

"You know, some things are more important than money." In Gabby's mind, that explained everything. Maybe it did.

Revenge did top the motive-for-murder list, but at the cost of damaging her own assets? Laughing all the way to the bank offered satisfaction, too.

We arrived at the Crown Ballroom, ending our discussion. Gabby's news did make me wonder if Ruby's Barkview visit included helping or hurting the brother's jewelry store.

In the ballroom, decorated in Diamonds Are Forever splendor, the candlelight cast an enchanting glow on the high-gloss paneling and silver-flecked topiaries overflowing with blush tea roses. Even the dinner tables sparkled with diamond-shaped confetti on the midnight-blue tablecloths.

Dinner came and went without incident. Chelsea caught me watching her and her father across the ballroom enough times to retaliate with a stare of her own. With Isaac and Jacob Samuels seated at the same table, how could I keep my eyes off it? That Jacob favored his arm throughout the event I also noted, as well as how different the brothers looked. Although they were dressed in similar black-and-white tuxedos, Jacob's tall, lithe frame turned heads, while Isaac seemed to be a wallflower. Both men did make a point of ignoring Ruby, who excitedly conversed with Angela at the GIA representative's table, her dog never moving from her lap.

With thirty-six hours remaining until the GIA officially took possession of the Shepard Diamond, the need to solve Chris's murder pressed down on me. A day and a half since Chris's murder, and I had so many dangling ideas, but no idea how they all fit together. In a room full of suspects, where did I even start?

When the dancing started and Logan Roma beelined it across the room, he confused me even more. He offered his uninjured arm to Stephanie, who hesitated only a moment before following him out on the dance floor. So much for ignoring him. The peaches-and-cream blush staining her otherwise pale complexion made her look radiant in a beaded forest-green dress. Her long hair was piled on her head and held in place with a diamond hair clip. Logan's nighttime visit to Stephanie's suddenly seemed less suspect.

"Stephanie is floating on air," Sandy said. Dressed in a knee-length black dress that showed off her long legs and athletic silhouette, she looked model-perfect.

No kidding. I'd never seen the Frosty Pups Creamery owner beam. Despite their height differences, Stephanie and Logan did seem to move as one. His stunning good looks contrasted yet melded with Stephanie's dark appeal. Everyone noticed it, especially Loreli, whose glare could have slashed metal. She cut in after a single song and promptly dragged her brother off the dance floor.

My something-big-was-going-down radar flared. I grabbed Russ's hand and dragged him onto the dance floor. "Get us close to Loreli and Logan. I want to hear what she's saying to him."

Russ didn't ask, he just moved us through the crowd and positioned us beside another overflowing floral topiary within conversation range.

"Stop it. You can't have her," Loreli snapped. Could this changeling really be sweet, biddable Loreli?

"I was dancing with her. Not marrying her." Logan's voice sounded childish.

"Grow up, dear brother. You have no choice. I'm tired of making excuses for you, and I'm tired of fixing everything." Loreli's arm gestured around the room.

Logan hunched his shoulders. He suddenly seemed a foot shorter. "I won't do it. I won't marry Sophia. I don't love her."

"Stop whining. It doesn't become you," Loreli continued more harshly. "What you want is of no consequence. Duty first. The bloodline must remain true."

“Easy for you to say. You don’t have to marry a cow.”

“True, brother.” Loreli laughed, and they disappeared into the crowd.

It all sounded so archaic. No one married out of duty anymore. Even Princes William and Harry had married for love. Why would Logan’s bloodline matter? And who was Sophia?

I’d known deep down that the past mattered in this investigation. Time to dig deeper. After I danced with Russ.

CHAPTER 17

Questions spun through my head despite the elegant surroundings. When the magnificent diamonds the GIA had sent over to complete our Shepard Diamond display failed to hold my attention, I knew I was on the verge of a breakthrough. Without thinking, I reached for my Post-it notes.

Russ caught my hand before I could do anything unrecoverable. His whisper was for my ears only. "Not here."

I know I flushed. Partially from being caught, but mostly because his warm breath tickled my bare neck. He was right. Pink Post-its would stand out against the linen tablecloth. The distraction faded fast, and I glanced around the room. I acknowledged a few greeting waves. How did Aunt Char handle the head-table fishbowl so effortlessly? I just felt boxed in. While my aunt flowed from one table to another, chatting easily with the guests, I only felt on display. A quick exit into the hotel would be noted by all the wrong people. Only one choice.

I clutched my purse as I stood. "I'm going to the ladies' room."

Russ rose with me and slipped me his pen. I almost busted out laughing. The man knew me far too well.

Sandy took my cue and followed. "What's up? I'm afraid to ask what you need a pen for."

So much for stealth. If Sandy had caught that exchange from across the table, who else had? The Barkview gossips would have their own spin. I couldn't worry about that now.

We entered the marble and gold-trimmed ladies' room. I headed for the larger handicapped stall and went right to work jotting down the name of each player involved in this convoluted investigation on individual notes. The wood-trimmed door turned out to be a perfect canvas. Chris Papas started my door collage, followed by Chelsea and Ty. Loreli and Logan, Madame Orr and Angela came next. Isaac Samuels's role in initiating the Shepard Diamond's loan via his jewelry store landed him a spot. Our former mayor, his deceased wife, and Firebird Industries current owner Victor Roma also made the cut. I stuck Chad and Stephanie to the far side. One look at that complex mess and I knew why my head had been spinning. The Shepard Diamond was the key. If I couldn't see Lynda's private papers, maybe Adam had left clues in his mayoral documents.

"You okay in there?" Sandy's concern snapped me out of it.

"I am. How long does it take for a dog to digest its food?" I removed each Post-it and crushed them into my beaded bag, flushed the toilet for effect and exited. Despite her impossibly narrow heels, Sandy stood ready for action, with her own tiny why-bother purse posed to defend.

"Depends on the dog. Jack, maybe twelve hours. A bigger dog could be two days. Why?"

Two days? That meant Gem had swallowed the diamond the same day Chris tried to steal the fake. I checked under the stall to confirm we were alone. "Up for a little sleuthing tonight?"

"Can I change first?" Eagerness glittered in her sapphire-blue eyes.

I nodded. How could I refuse? The plunging back of her dress didn't exactly bring stealth to mind. She removed a needle from the ladies' room accessory tray and popped a seam on her hem. "Wardrobe malfunction. Time to go home."

I laughed along with her, not really thinking about why she did it until we returned to the table and her date jumped to her aid. She'd neatly avoided any objections.

Sandy hugged me as they prepared to leave. "Give me an hour. Where do you want me to meet you?"

"Employee entrance at City Hall." I swear Russ's ears twitched. Before he could ask, I added, "Deniability is a good thing."

No argument; he simply handed me his car keys. "I'd prefer to stay with the Shepard Diamond tonight. I'll come by tomorrow and pick up the car." He put his hand out for his pen and kissed my cheek.

This man's keeper points just kept coming. I really needed to add them all up after I solved this mess.

I drove Russ's Land Rover back to my place. Gem did not greet me at the door. Her expressive ears popped up in acknowledgment while her eyes remained fixed on the drooping succulent on the countertop. Housing a diamond wasn't helping that plant any.

I scratched her head as I walked by, ignoring the floating fur fluffs, and quickly changed into sneak-around black leggings and a sweatshirt. Then I dug beneath my workout clothes in my bottomless dresser drawer until I found the cool-spy-stuff fanny pack I'd put together during my very first investigation. My neck scar throbbed in memory of the resulting dog attack, but for the most part, I'd come to terms with those painful memories. I even had a German Shepherd in my house. Who'd have thought that even a few years ago?

I unzipped the pack and removed the picklock kit and pen camera/recorder. The cool sunglass camera, key-copying kit, and popcorn kernel–size bugging device could wait for another adventure. Who knew you could buy all that secret agent stuff online, no questions asked?

I repacked my equipment into another bag already containing baggies and gloves. Bringing Gem for protection made sense, but that telltale fur trail gave me pause. Besides, how dangerous could City Hall be at 2 a.m.? I peeked at the sad succulent on my counter protecting the priceless treasure. Did I dare leave it unguarded?

In the end, stealth won, and I left Gem behind. I drove Russ's car back to the village and parked in the police station parking lot next door. I looked carefully around before exiting into the fog and walking around back to the City Hall employee entrance. Sandy jogged up a few minutes later. She was dressed all in black, her blonde hair covered in a dark beanie; we looked like a pair of cat burglars on the prowl.

"So, what's the plan?" she asked.

I admired her Jack-Russell enthusiasm even more so tonight, after an endless day of party prep followed by the event. "I need your help to get into Ty's computer."

Her frown didn't help my confidence any. "That may not be so easy."

"You broke into Jan's computer in, like, a minute." Sandy had seriously impressed me the day she'd figured out the murdered librarian's computer password in no time.

"Ty doesn't have a Jack Russell handy."

True, the dog's collar had spelled it out for us. There still had to be a way in. "I know Aunt Char's passwords." At least I thought I did. "Since Ty's system is connected to hers..."

"There may be a way to piggyback in through the server." Sandy finished my thought for me, her tone hopeful. I took that as a good sign.

I unlocked the Victorian's solid wood door with my key to Aunt Char's office. No need for complete stealth. Barkview City Council's no-surveillance-camera rule applied to City Hall. Unless someone saw us, we'd be in the clear.

The door clicked shut behind us, setting my nerves on edge. In a building normally bustling with activity, the acute silence made our footsteps sound like a stampede as we crossed the parquet floor to the English oak staircase. I caught myself tiptoeing to avoid disturbing the almost uneasy stillness, periodically interrupted by an old building groan. Once upstairs, antique wall sconces illuminated our path to the mayor's office fronting Oak Street.

I unlocked Aunt Char's outer office door and felt along the wall for the light switch. Since the reception area occupied an interior room, lights wouldn't be seen from outside. I pressed the switch to on. Once. Twice. Nothing happened. My heartbeat spiked. No need to panic yet. Hundred-year-old electrical wiring could be finicky. I pressed the switch more firmly. Still nothing. Had someone cut the power? No. The hall lights were on.

Suddenly, something demonic jumped out at me. I stumbled backward, nearly plowing over Sandy as a monster with flailing arms lunged at me. I dragged her with me behind one of the padded straight-backed waiting-room chairs as the lights flickered, then held. To my chagrin, the attacker turned out to be the coat tree alongside Ty's desk. Sandy didn't laugh either, telling me she'd been equally as spooked. A minute later, she slipped into Ty's desk chair.

I handed her a pair of disposable gloves from my pack. No sense leaving evidence of our little information-gathering mission behind. I typed in Aunt Char's password. My second attempt worked, proving people did use familiar and personally significant information in passwords. Note to self: get more creative with passwords.

"Exactly what am I looking for?" Sandy whispered.

Why I whispered in return made no sense. No one could hear us. "I want to know everything you can find on the Shepard Diamond and Firebird Industries. Ty had access to Adam Smythe's mayoral records. Somehow he's involved in this."

Sandy frowned. "A better source might be the former mayor's archived files."

"Heading to the City Records Room now." With any luck, Adam Smythe had referenced something sensitive in meeting notes or on a calendar.

Sandy waved me aside. "Go do whatever you do that I don't want to know about."

With that vote of confidence, I left her to do her thing. City records were stored on the lower level. I'd visited the file box storage area many times in pursuit of news-related research. There were no real secrets in there, just as there was nothing illegal about looking at the records that interested me. Just the timing. Waiting until Monday's regular business hours wasn't an option. The Shepard Diamond had to be returned before the GIA authenticated the stone.

Just call me a snoop. My not-too-rusty skills picked the door lock in a single try. I peered into the still room, illuminated by a greenish computer screen glow, before entering. A wooden bench lined the right wall, which faced a granite counter fronting a long corridor stacked floor to ceiling on both sides with white file boxes. I ignored the client-facing computer screen and entered the file box corridor. Since there were no windows, I switched on the overhead lights and quickly scanned the box labels. Adam was old school. With any luck, he'd scribbled in date books and on margins.

I found the boxes containing mayoral records a few minutes later on the top shelf. Of course. I pulled over a step stool and climbed up. The box felt light, too light. Instead of climbing down, I lifted the lid and peeked in. Furballs! It was empty. Someone had beaten me to it, but who? And when? Had I alerted Chelsea tonight? No way she'd gotten here first. Ty, on the other hand, had sped away in plenty of time. He also had a key.

As a last resort, I flipped through the record room's sign-in logbook on the countertop. Sure, the culprit could've snuck in as I had, but it was worth a look. Madame Orr's signature jumped right out at me. What could the psychic possibly need to find in Barkview's city records? The day, Tuesday, set off alarms, too. The water main break occurred on Tuesday, the same day the series of events leading to Chris's murder had started. Coincidence? Not a chance.

The hairs on my neck tingled as I hurried up the staircase. Like it or not, the clues kept leading to Madame Orr. Ugh. Only a compelling reason would encourage that woman to share information. I needed something big to take back to her.

Hopefully, Sandy had been more successful. I heard her feverish typing as I approached Ty's office.

"Someone is remotely deleting files," she shouted, even before I crossed the threshold.

"That's possible?" It happened in the movies all the time, but in real life?

"Yeah." She hammered away on the keys, finally throwing her hands up. Sandy defeated? A first.

"Did you get anything?" I had to ask.

"A broken nail." Sandy flopped back in the chair and pouted. "Someone totally knew we were coming."

In retrospect, maybe stalking Chelsea at the gala hadn't been a good plan. "So, Adam Smythe is involved." Deep down, I'd thought so. But why? "Is it possible to track who did the deleting?"

"Maybe Russ can." Sandy snapped off the gloves. "What did you find in records?"

"The box was empty."

Sandy's *hmmm* didn't inspire excitement. "So, our prior mayor was involved."

"He knew something someone wants to hide," I said.

"What are we missing?"

I'd been asking myself that same question for days. "I wish I knew. The argument between Ty and Chelsea has to be relevant. Were they involved?"

"Involved in what?" Sandy asked.

"Dating?"

Sandy almost choked on her laugh. "What makes you think that?"

"The way Gabby described Ty's reaction to their argument."

"Consider the source," Sandy said.

Point taken. The gossip queen did tend to embellish to improve the story.

"Ty is hardly Chelsea's type. Gabby will know more details, but I heard Chelsea's boyfriend is a partner at her San Francisco law firm."

No doubt another lawyer would be more her style. Could she have used Ty to get information by having him spy on Aunt Char? But still, why? What could either Smythe hope to gain? It was the same question I couldn't answer about Madame Orr.

CHAPTER 18

Russ met me on my beachside patio at 9 a.m., carrying my favorite caramel cappuccino and two acai bowls, adding to his already impressive keeper tally. I added another point when I got a whiff of pure espresso seeping from his extra-large cup. He'd been up all night, yet had taken the time to shower and change into jeans and a shoulder-emphasizing navy shirt before coming over.

I, on the other hand, had just crawled out of bed. My crumpled leopard pajama bottoms and up-all-night red eyes made me look like Gem had run me through a tornado. So much for following Aunt Char's prepared-for-any-encounter training. At least I'd brushed my teeth.

I bit back a snarky comment, instead lacing my fingers around the warm cup. The first long swallow of coffee helped temper my growl. I leaned against the patio table and looked out over the sand. It was too early to see the surf through the morning fog, but I did hear it rolling ashore.

"Twenty-four hours and counting until the GIA takes possession of the Shepard Diamond." His jaw tightened.

My eye strayed inside my townhouse toward the succulent hiding the real stone. I couldn't help it. Should I tell him not to worry? His legal responsibilities still applied. "I take it no one tried to break in?" The whole idea had been a long shot anyway. Chris's killer knew the stone was a fake.

"Too quiet. I doubt the thieves will try again."

I readjusted my bangs. "What if the plan all along was to embarrass Aunt Char?"

"Or Blue Diamond," Russ added.

I hadn't even considered that angle. Blue Diamond Security always seemed so untouchable. Call me oblivious! Only Adam Smythe's possible motives had occurred to me.

Russ took another long swallow of his coffee. "An elaborate plan involving multiple federal charges to get a small town mayor recalled?"

Verbalized, it sounded ridiculous. "Will the Shepard Diamond's theft hurt your company's reputation?" The "elaborate plan" part resonated. Orchestrating the intricate series of events had taken a lot of money.

"Not significantly. We don't normally play in the jewelry security business."

Last time Russ would do a favor for Uncle G. I noted a large running group approaching and waved him inside. He greeted Gem with a fur-exploding pet.

Gem's ears perked to majestic points as Russ let out rapid-fire sneezes yet continued to stroke her. I dust-busted around him. Not that it did any good. Only twenty-four hours and counting to find Chris's killer. He must've figured the sneezing was worth it.

I pointed Russ toward my dining room table covered in multicolored Post-it notes detailing our investigation to date. While some would call it a suspect board, linking suspects and events, I just liked to visualize the connections. Russ scratched his chin as he took a long, hard look. Anticipation hummed through him at the same tempo as mine. In so many ways we were well-suited. In others...not so much. He was a stickler for following the rules, so my improvised end-justifies-the-means attitude pushed his buttons. Any wonder "painful" described confessing to my early morning sleuthing with Sandy at City Hall? I'd seriously considered not mentioning it at all, but the need to know who had deleted the files made tolerating his lecture bearable.

Oddly, Russ only took another swig of coffee.

"I didn't do anything illegal." I couldn't keep the defensiveness from creeping out. When the man drank straight caffeine in a search for calmness, trouble brewed.

"No? How about criminal trespass and revelation of confidential matters for the computer access? On second thought, don't tell me how you accessed Adam Smythe's records."

No doubt he'd already guessed anyway. "I have a key and the prior mayor's records are all public."

"I challenge you to find a DA who agrees."

My cappuccino suddenly curdled. "I didn't gather any information."

"By sheer luck." Russ jabbed a plastic spoon into the acai bowl. "What if someone had been there?" He stirred. "Do you have no concern for your safety?"

His concern warmed me. His anger stemmed from the risks I took, not entirely about the rules.

"At least you had Gem to protect you," he said.

I didn't correct him. Gem's ears puffed to Yoda-size and then flattened back. Outed by my supposed protector. Good thing Russ didn't speak Gem's language. Wait, did I?

It took me a second to refocus. "The point is, someone deleted all of Adam Smythe's files."

"That is suspect, I agree."

"I also discovered that Madame Orr signed into the records room on Tuesday morning."

"Before the water main break?" Russ connected the dots quickly. I liked that about him.

"Yup. Wanna come interrogate her with me?"

Russ's grin sent tingles down my spine. Only another true investigator would find my request exciting. "Give me a few hours to look into the deleted files and do a deep dive into Madame Orr."

"And Angela Cooper. Gabby saw her meet with Madame Orr too."

Russ agreed as Sandy's Jack Russell shot through my patio door, barking like a lunatic and dragging her with him. Jack darted right under my coffee table, jerking the leash out of her hand. Free, he hurdled the swivel chair next to it and sailed into the kitchen, skidding across the travertine floor until he plowed into Gem's solid chest. Jack's yelp came out as a squeak.

My breath caught. We all held our breath waiting for Gem's next move. Surprisingly, she didn't make a sound or turn Sandy's terrier into a one-bite snack. Ears twitching to the sky, the dog shook her regal head and peered down her nose like a seasoned matron until Jack whimpered and scooted behind Sandy, his tail between his legs.

Dressed in running shorts and a Bark U sweatshirt with her long hair tied back in a low ponytail, Sandy looked anything but overtired; her peaches and cream complexion glowed. "That will teach you, you terrorist."

"Hardly," I muttered. Russ heard me. He nudged me. "Disaster averted," I said louder. "Running by?" I needed a shot of her endless energy today.

"Running here. I found something." She paused for effect. "In-ter-esting."

My pulse thumped. She'd had me at "found something." Both Russ and I watched as she stripped off her backpack and removed her iPad. The paper pile that followed had to be for my benefit, since Sandy lived on the screen. She left Jack in the kitchen and headed toward the mess on my dining room table before pivoting to the granite breakfast counter that separated my kitchen from the living area. My heart almost stopped when she stepped over Gem and reached for the succulent. I stopped Gem from growling just in time as Sandy resettled the plant on the counter beside the sink. Gem took a new position defending the plant in this location.

Another disaster averted. Russ and I crowded around Sandy. She laid out a family tree with Logan and Loreli's names circled at the bottom. The complicated branches all started with the marriage of Sophia of Dalsia in 1894. This couldn't be the same Sophia Logan had been discussing.

"Am I looking at Victor Roma's family tree?" Trust Russ to make no assumptions.

"Yes. On the surface it looks pretty normal until you look at the pedigree of all the spouses. Two royal princesses, a Scottish duchess whose mother was a direct descendant of Queen Victoria, and a Russian grand duchess who was a first cousin to Nicholas II."

"Russia hasn't had an aristocracy since 1917," I said.

"The aristocracy isn't ruling, but the families who survived the Bolshevik revolution still carry the titles." Sandy's explanation made too much sense.

"Am I understanding that Logan Roma is a prince?" Russ asked.

Sandy nodded. "A descendant of Dalsian, Russian, Romanian, and British royalty, yes. His maternal grandfather was the last king of Romania."

I collapsed into the barstool. "How do you know this?"

"I followed the leaf." As if that explained anything. My confusion couldn't be entirely related to my lack of sleep. Russ's frown questioned her as well.

"I did an online genealogy search through that ancestry company that's always advertising. I traced the Roma family back to a grandfather born in 1894 in Dalsia."

She answered before I could ask.

"It's a small country between Spain and Portugal. They are known for growing cork and cross-breeding Akhal-Teke and Andalusian horses. The show horses are beautiful. Before cars, the horses could be found in most royal stables."

"There's nothing before 1894?"

"Only on the mother's side. I called a friend of mine who's a genealogy junkie."

Of course Sandy had a friend she could call on Sunday morning for help. I really did have the best assistant ever.

"She couldn't find anything either. She did caution me that birth records could've been destroyed in a fire or during the Spanish Civil War, when the communists occupied Dalsia. My friend did find a listing in the Dalsian royal family's Bible proclaiming them as legit though."

"Does that mean Logan is a royal?" Never a royal watcher myself, the protocol eluded me.

"It sure does. He is a direct descendant of the Dalsian royal family through Princess Sophia of Dalsia. The odd part is that his father's name appears to be scratched out or damaged."

"Who did Princess Sophia marry?" How hard could that info be to find?

"There's nothing in recorded history. The marriage is recorded in the Bible, but, again, the man's name is illegible. There's a good chance the man was Russian and noble because Princess Sophia converted to Russian Orthodoxy three months prior to the wedding in January 1894."

"Is Princess Sophia's son still considered a prince?" Russ asked.

"Yes. In fact, Princess Sophia had twins. A boy and a girl. They were born nine months from the date of the wedding. The girl's name was Maria Natasha."

"A Slavic name in a Latin country?" I asked.

"Another weird thing in a long list of them," Sandy remarked. "What I do know is Logan and Loreli are blue-blooded royals with blood ties to the Russian royal family."

I shared a glance with Russ. The conversation we'd overheard last night between Logan and Loreli suddenly made perfect sense. But what did it matter? Communism replaced monarchy in Russia over a hundred years ago. "This is all interesting, but..."

"I thought so, too, until..." Sandy shuffled through the pile of papers, finally handing me a newspaper article. "I discovered that there is a well-financed movement in Russia to reinstate the monarchy."

In a country ruled by communism for four generations? I read the article translated from a Moscow paper anyway. More than thirty percent of Russians would support a restoration of the monarchy? Had to be a typo. "That'll never happen," I announced. The revolutionaries wiped out the entire royal family in 1918. A DNA test had even debunked Anastasia's claim.

"That is what history says. What if history is wrong?" Sandy asked.

"The financial implications of property and jewelry alone are staggering," Russ added.

Russ had been too quiet during Sandy's explanation. Did he buy any of this? Was it even possible? My overtired brain couldn't take it in. The political implications would be staggering. I couldn't image the ruling communist party going down quietly. Were we talking another revolution in the second-most-powerful superpower in the world?

Russ always said to follow the money. Sure, the palaces and riches in places like the gold room in Saint Petersburg equaled motive—a whole lot of motive—but what was world political dominance worth?

"True, and in Russia only a male heir of noble descent can accede to the throne," Sandy added.

"Every Russian noble had to marry another noble?" That couldn't be an extensive gene pool. No wonder hemophilia had struck.

"They could marry outside the circle, but their children couldn't inherit. Logan's line is..."

"Pure by definition, starting in 1894. Unless Great-Great-Grandpa Nicholas's father was a commoner," Sandy admitted.

It still didn't make sense. "What happened in Russian and European history in 1894?"

Sandy typed on her iPad. "Quite a lot. Nicholas II inherited the Russian throne. On November 11, he married Queen Victoria's granddaughter, Alix of Hesse."

I still couldn't believe it. "For laughs, say you're right about a Russian desire to restore the monarchy. Who's the next in line?"

"That's the problem. When the Bolsheviks assassinated Czar Nicholas and his entire family, they ended seven hundred years of Romanov rule. His sister's descendants don't meet the legal requirements."

"But if there was a male heir..."

"Story of King Henry VIII." Sandy's quip did hit home. "Seriously, there aren't any. Nicholas's uncle would be the next logical choice, but that side of the line has lost any claim to a title."

"Meaning they didn't marry appropriately?" I asked.

"Yup. By definition, there are no legal heirs."

No doubt to Putin's pleasure. "So, the return to the monarchy is a farce." My imagination suddenly went wild. "What if Nicholas did have another son? A child born before he married Alix..."

Sandy's kid-in-the-candy-store expression faded. "That's doubtful. History says Nicholas wasn't a philanderer. Although there's a conspiracy theory he may have fathered a child with a ballet dancer before his marriage, it wouldn't matter. That child could not legally inherit."

"What if he did marry and had an heir?" I asked.

"He'd have been a bigamist. Besides, Nicholas and Alix were a love match. History tells us that Nicholas fell madly in love with her years before they married, but Alix kept turning down his proposals. In fact, she did again in April 1894, when he was in Germany attending Alix's brother's wedding. The bride was Nicholas's cousin."

That got my attention. "And Kaiser Wilhelm's too?"

"Royalty was all related. Why?"

"There's no record of an eighty-carat yellow diamond coming out of the British South African mines. The German South African mines were not as strictly run and pilferage remained high," I explained.

"You think Nicholas purchased it from the Kaiser?" We were on the same page.

"Maybe to impress Alix."

"If he tried to convince her with it, it didn't work. She turned him down again."

"Perhaps he gave the diamond to someone else."

Russ's sneeze brought me back to reality. "I'll let you two meander into fantasyland." I handed him his keys.

"Whoever deleted those files..."

"I'm on it. I'll call you in a few hours." Russ exited through the garage door. I returned to find Gem growling at Sandy, blocking her from moving toward the succulent. "That plant is far too pathetic for Gem to defend."

I should've known Sandy would figure it out. Did I dare tell? "I needed to give her something to guard. She was driving me crazy."

Disbelief showed in Sandy's raised brow.

"There are things you don't want to know."

"Like why you're hiding a priceless diamond in plain sight," Sandy stated.

No sense denying the truth. "Got a better idea? We don't know who killed Chris or if it was an inside GIA job. I have a feeling if I give back the diamond now, we'll never know."

Sandy nodded. "Point made. What's the next step?"

I took another look at the Roma family tree. Victor's sister, Natasha Anna Maria Koratova, popped up at me. Could it be that simple? "Can you find out if Natasha Koratova legally changed her name, and when?"

Sandy referred to her iPad. "There are a few sites. It might take a while. OMG."

I froze. "It's Madame Orr, isn't it?"

"Yup. Three years ago, Madame Orr legally changed her name."

No wonder she'd visited Barkview City Records. "Want to bet her original business license is missing?"

"She is Victor Roma's sister," Sandy said. "Bet Adam Smythe knew it too since Firebird Industries bought his family's company."

I reorganized my Post-its on the dining room table. The pieces finally started to make sense. "She's also Logan and Loreli's aunt." I headed for my bedroom. It was time for Gem to check out Logan. Prince or not, if he'd gone after the Shepard Diamond and killed Chris, he'd pay for it.

CHAPTER 19

I arrived at the Old Barkview Inn thirty minutes later, ten minutes behind schedule since Gem decided my original jeans and an oversized sweatshirt weren't appropriate attire. She finally quit shaking her head when I put on black slacks and a blue-gray V-neck sweater that complimented my eyes. I didn't even try to wear comfy court shoes, but opted for my navy boots on the first try. Why she cared what I wore bothered me less than why I cared what she thought at all.

Security remained tight in front of the Crown Ballroom housing the Shepard Diamond display. I counted two armed officers standing outside as I entered the lobby. I also figured Max and Maxine guarded the inside since I'd seen Uncle G's SUV in valet parking. No wonder the thieves hadn't retried to steal the diamond. The task looked impossible.

I waved to the officer on duty as I headed to the Otis elevator with Gem shadowing my heels. After two days, I hardly noticed her any longer. I did feel a sense of security I hadn't felt in years. Odd. I'd always thought freedom was my number one driver. Now, I wasn't so sure.

Will slid open the iron doors, his Victorian dress uniform in starched order. He greeted Gem with his usual smile. "Good morning, Miss Wright and Miss Gem. Mr. Logan and Miss Loreli are checking out this afternoon."

No doubt Loreli's decision after Logan's behavior last night. "I would like to wish them safe travels," I said. "Has Madame Orr been to see them yet?"

Will inclined his head. "She left ten minutes ago down the back stairs."

As if anyone could escape Will's hawk-eyes. "How often has she come by?"

"I am aware of three visits." Although his facial expression did not change, I noted Will's disapproval.

"Maybe they had more to discuss than spirits."

Will nodded. "One can only hope."

I thanked him as I exited the elevator and headed toward the Oxford Suite. If I expected Gem to do something I could interpret as aggressive, she disappointed me. Her ears were upright but didn't even twitch as we approached the suite. I knocked twice before Loreli opened the door. Tessa peeked her head out and jerked back, striking Loreli's shins.

"Oh. Hi, Cat." She picked up Tessa the moment she saw Gem. "Uh. We're just packing to leave."

Prisms seemed to float around Tessa, all centered on the pavé diamond J Tracker collar. "Wow. Tessa's collar is stunning," I said.

"Your aunt's dog has the same collar."

"True, but Tessa's coloring shows it off well." Listen to me talking dog fashion.

Loreli blushed. "I know. The tricolor Cavalier is..."

Ugh. Another fanatic. I waited until she took a breath before interrupting. "Why did you buy the multicolored collar like Gem's?" I'd stunned her with that bit of info.

"How did you...? It's not important. The collar was a gift. Colored stones are the thing for white dogs."

"No kidding?" What else could I say? I knew little about fashion, for dogs or otherwise.

As if she'd said too much, Loreli changed the subject. "We really are short on time."

"I understand. I just need a word with Logan," I said quickly.

Afraid she'd close the door on my foot, I nudged Gem forward. Loreli stepped aside as the dog nosed her way in. I followed, hoping for some sign. Gem just sat in the entry, facing the suite's living room. She looked to the left toward Logan's room, her ears alert, but made no further move, aggressive or otherwise.

According to Gem, Logan hadn't killed Chris. But with a dog bite and no alibi, he'd been such a promising suspect. Could the dog be wrong? She had been drugged.

"Logan, Cat is here to see you." Loreli took a last look at Gem and carried Tessa to safety in the room on the right. I noticed several suitcases on the bed, supporting her comment about packing, before she shut the door.

Maybe Logan's dog bite had been one big misunderstanding. I had a hard time understanding Stephanie's surfer lingo sometimes, too, and I lived on the beach in the midst of the culture.

Logan strolled out of his room, cradling his bandaged forearm. Dressed in Dockers and a blue polo that matched his eyes, he should have swept me off my feet with his uncanny charm. Instead, an ever-so slight hunch in his shoulders drew my eye. "Are you okay?"

"I'll be fine. What can I do for you?" He reached out to scratch Gem. "Beautiful Shepherd. I didn't take you for a dog person."

He'd read that one right. Gem cocked her head to give him better access to her ears. No way she'd allow Chris's killer to touch her so familiarly. I breathed easier. Deep down, I didn't want him to be the killer. Time to fill in some of the blanks.

"Shall I call you 'Your Highness?'"

"Excuse me?" His eyes darted everywhere but at me.

"I know why you're here." I pushed harder.

He sank into the nearest chair and rubbed his forehead. "How did you find out?"

So it was true! "I'm an investigative reporter." As if that said it all.

He didn't question a thing. "Apparently a very good one." He glanced toward Loreli's room and whispered, "Does Stephanie know?"

"No."

"Please tell her I am sorry. It cannot be between us." Resignation shone in his eyes. Louder, he said, "I told Loreli hanging around here was a mistake. Too many people know about the Shepard Diamond."

"Why did you come here?"

"We wanted to see it," Loreli said from the doorway. An avenging angel came to mind, the way her flowing blouse appeared to be wings.

"The Shepard Diamond was on display at the Smithsonian," I said.

"Under government surveillance," Logan added.

Not the answer I expected. Painful as it was, I crossed my arms and waited for them to continue. It worked. Logan spoke. "No one can know who I am."

"It's not safe," Loreli added quickly. She rested her hands on her brother's shoulder. "They would kill him if they knew."

I yoga-breathed. I wanted to ask who "they" were, but

figured I'd better wait for Logan to explain. He seemed ready to burst anyway.

"I'm safe until we have the documents. Right now, I'm just one more Anastasia."

Suddenly the crazy supposition Sandy and I made earlier seemed possible. "How do you expect to be restored to power?"

"I don't know that I can be. Uncle Victor believes that a legitimate heir will rally the populace."

Rally fourth-generation communists behind a king? "What do you think?"

"That the monarchy died over a hundred years ago." Logan's perception seemed right on.

"A constitutional monarchy..." Loreli chimed in.

"Is non-ruling. It's ceremonial only." The clarification characterized Logan's feelings exactly. I saw it in his eyes.

"But not without influence," Loreli insisted.

A common argument between the two, I could tell, when Logan took a deep breath. "It's a high personal price to pay for ribbon cutting. I look at the British monarchy and—"

"Shudder." I filled in that blank.

"Exactly. And a long-lost czar? It'd be a media circus."

No kidding. The twins currently avoided that at all costs. To a very small degree, I related. Even Aunt Char's small-town mayoral status chafed at times. I couldn't image their situation. "I don't envy you one bit."

Logan shook his head. "I half hope the prophecy isn't true and the Douglas Diamond is never found."

"No, brother, your destiny has been written for one hundred and twenty years."

"Even if the Douglas Diamond is found, you still need the Shepard Diamond," I pointed out. "Right now, it's still a US government treasure."

I caught the twins' shared glance. I'd missed something.

Loreli moved right in, her calculating look saying it all. "You'll need to speak with Tetya Anna. Come, brother, we must go. We would ask that you do not share this information with anyone. You will put our lives in danger."

Tell a reporter not to report? And a story of this magnitude had Pulitzer written all over it. Still...of course, I wouldn't put them in danger. "When the time is right, we'll talk again." When I found the Douglas Diamond, they'd have no choice.

"I've no doubt. Destiny is following us both," Loreli said.

Gem and I left on that note. Destiny just kept coming at me. Too bad wallowing in that future did nothing to find Chris's killer. Since Gem had cleared Logan, it was time to see Madame Orr again. If the prophecy required both the Shepard and Douglas Diamonds to fulfill it, I'd finally discovered the motive.

CHAPTER 20

Madame Orr, dressed in nondescript slacks and a café-au-lait sweater, with her lamb-dog plastered to her side, greeted Russ, Gem, and me from the porch. Thanks to Loreli's fashion sense, the twinkling multi-gem collar did make that odd-looking terrier seem more doglike.

"I've been expecting you," Madame Orr said.

Russ's comforting hand on the small of my back relaxed me enough to shake off my trepidation. I'd infiltrated the Romas' secret circle. No doubt the twins had warned her. Truth be told, Russ had, too, after his deep dive into the family. My revelations hadn't surprised him at all. If we'd figured it out, how many others had too?

The lack of news on the file-deleting culprits bothered me the most. Someone who knew what they were doing had initiated it. Although Russ seemed confident his team would eventually locate answers, I wasn't so sure. The higher the stakes, the better the cover-up was the rule that applied here.

Gem led the way, her ears alert, not laid back in threat mode. I felt better already. I'd insisted she accompany us. Not because I doubted Russ's ability to protect or read Madame Orr, but to be warned if reinforcements had been called in. Based on Gem's alert but nonaggressive reaction, I surmised no imminent threat. That I understood Gem bothered me even more. Who'd believe I could ever understand a guard dog?

Russ took in the psychic's parlor in a sweeping no-emotion, threat-assessing glance. I had to love that. On my last visit, the parlor had been set with two straight-backed chairs and a table. This time, three cozy chairs encircled a round coffee table laid with a dainty floral Haviland tea service, a matching bowl for Gem, a small, carved wooden box with a Moorish motif, and a pink Post-it notepad with a pen. Maybe her psychic skills were real.

The meticulously-set scene did not affect Russ. When his hand no longer hovered over his concealed weapon, I relaxed. Madame Orr saw it too.

"Now that you realize I am not a threat, please be seated." We sat down, Gem so close she pressed against my calf and crushed my right foot.

Madame Orr poured our tea, adding a splash of coconut milk to mine and cream to Russ's without asking. "Let me start by saying I did not kill Christos Papas. I hired him to cut an exact replica of the Shepard Diamond, which he delivered to me on Tuesday morning." She removed a glittering yellow diamond from the wooden box and handed the stone and a loupe to Russ. The second replica had been found.

Russ held the stone to the light and then passed it me.

"It is a near-perfect replica," Madame Orr stated.

"Near-perfect?" Golden prisms flashed across the table like rays of morning sunshine, so like the real stone's brilliance the naked eye couldn't tell the difference. I should know; I'd now inspected both.

"The Shepard Diamond is graded as flawless, which technically means there are no blemishes or inclusion visible at 10X magnification."

I knew that, thanks to more of those GIA diamond education classes I'd taken.

"If you look at 30X magnification on the real stone, you will see an ever-so-slight blemish modern technology could not duplicate," Madame Orr continued.

I glanced at the offered GIA report and made a note of the location to check.

"I assure you, this is synthetic. Here is the receipt for the lab-created rough." She handed Russ an invoice. Over his shoulder, I recognized the Cyrillic letters. Russian from the look of it.

I didn't want to believe her, but I did. So did Russ, judging from his pressed lips.

This required a whole lot of planning. A rough the exact color of the Shepard Diamond would take weeks to create. "How did you get the right color rough?"

"I don't know. Victor handled the rough purchase through Samuels and Sons," she explained.

In an instant we came full circle to Ariana and Chris's competition. "Why Samuels and Sons?" I had to ask.

"They had the relationship with the rough dealer."

I shared an on-the-same-page glance with Russ. Firebird Industries purchasing Samuels and Sons now made perfect sense. And there was only one reason I could name for a high-end jewelry store to cultivate a relationship with a fake diamond producer. This wasn't the first diamond replica Samuels and Sons had commissioned. I scribbled on a Post-it note and crammed it into my pocket.

"Where did you get the diamond-grading report?" No way Chris had cut the stones without it. The report had to have been provided months ago to make the rough in time.

"My grandfather had a GIA report done before he donated the diamond to the Smithsonian."

"You mean 'sold it.'" You couldn't call the stash of currency diamonds he'd traded for it anything else than a sale.

Madame Orr shrugged. "Bartered."

Fair enough. "If you knew all along you would need the diamond back, why sell it?"

"Grandpa V called it his biggest mistake. He really had no choice. He was destitute when he finally escaped from Romania. The NKVD, the Russian secret police back then, were after him. The Soviets somehow found out he had a yellow diamond, so he needed to hide it someplace safe. Someplace he could get it back from when we were ready for it."

"He chose a federal museum?"

"The gem's safety was his first concern. Back then, laboratory-grown diamonds weren't an option. He needed to know where the stone was and provide for its safety. The US government seemed like the best option."

"What is Angela's role?" I asked. She had to be involved.

"The 1958 GIA report wasn't as precise as they are today. Chris needed the most current report."

"Angela arranged it for you?"

"My brother, Victor, loaned his extensive amber collection to the GIA for exhibition," Madame Orr explained.

"Bribery," I said.

"Nothing illegal about it."

She was right. "Of all the diamond cutters in the world, why did you choose Chris?"

Madame Orr replied without hesitation. "Lynda Smythe recommended him."

Lynda Smythe again. The woman had passed away six months ago. She couldn't possibly be involved. Yet she had something to do with this—I just knew it.

"Why did Lynda Smythe see you?" I asked.

Madame Orr pinched the bridge of her nose, allowing silence to stretch between us. Finally, she said, "Lynda came to me looking for a spiritual adviser."

"Lynda is now deceased." Was Madame Orr's hesitation professional or private in nature? A priest's confessional oath hardly applied here.

"The full truth will eventually come out. Ambition drove that woman. She came to me to contact her grandmother."

"And did you?"

"The woman never showed herself," she admitted.

"Yet you kept trying." I couldn't help the dryness that crept into my voice. Another psychic trick to hook the hopeful.

"I told Lynda it wasn't happening, but she insisted I keep trying. It made no sense until Lynda let slip that Marie Douglas was her great-aunt."

Lynda Smythe had longtime ties to Barkview? Could it get any more twisted? "Marie was from France."

"Marie's mother opened a dress shop in Barkview in 1918. Jonathan met her when he returned from the trenches. They say it was love at first sight. Marie married Jonathan. Her sister married a businessman and settled in Louisiana. Lynda felt a kinship to the missing diamond."

"More like she had a need for the publicity surrounding it," I added.

Madame Orr's smile snuck out. "Lynda had her eye on the governor's mansion."

"You, of course, told her she'd get there."

The psychic's crooked half-smile sent a chill down my spine. "I may have admitted that a Barkview mayor will someday be governor."

"Governor of what?" Any flippancy fell flat. A vision of Aunt

Char on the State Capitol steps in Sacramento about floored me.

Madame Orr's smile widened. "Your intuition is quite accurate. Do use it wisely."

A warning or a compliment? I wasn't sure. Russ pulled me out of that rabbit hole by refocusing the conversation. "The job was too important to rely on one recommendation. Who else did you ask about Chris Papas?"

Madame Orr's gaze lingered a moment longer on me before she responded. "Victor vetted Chris's references and approved his hire."

"I'd like the names," Russ said.

Madame Orr inclined her head. "I will ask Victor."

"Why did you provide two diamond roughs to his exact requirements?" I asked.

"Chris insisted, in case one wasn't suitable."

"You didn't think that was odd?" Russ asked.

"The man was an artist. I liked his thoroughness. Timing was more important and obtaining a rough of that quality was time-consuming. I couldn't afford a mistake."

"You expect me to believe you provided two roughs to a jewel thief and you asked no questions?"

"A jewel thief?" Her voice cracked. She hadn't known. "He was an award-winning diamond cutter and goldsmith. Victor approved him too," Madame Orr insisted.

"No doubt with Adam Smythe's recommendation," I added.

"Yes, I believe so, and Isaac Samuels's."

Isaac recommending his competitor to cut a rough he'd obtained seemed out of character. Surely, past experience offered another option. If he and the prior mayor had been working together... Had the Smythes known about Chris's past?

Adam's brother was high up in the FBI. But Chris and Ariana were in witness protection, administered by the US Marshals. At some point all the clues had to come together. Right?

"I'm finding it hard to believe that a diamond replica completes the prophecy." If Madame Orr hadn't orchestrated the jewel heist, who had? I was running out of suspects.

"But it does. The Shepard and Douglas Diamonds together are needed to unlock the proof."

"They're keys?"

"Of sorts." Madame Orr's eyes shimmered like perfect brown diamonds.

"What does that mean?" Russ asked.

"The priest's marriage record was hidden for safekeeping. The two stones together will reveal the location."

It didn't take a psychic to see our skepticism, but she continued, "The story goes that Princess Sophia of Dalsia met Nicholas and Kaiser Wilhelm when the men came to Dalsia on a horse-breeding expedition in 1893. Sophia fell madly in love with Nicholas.

"Nicholas returned to Dalsia in January of 1894. Alix of Hesse had again rejected his marriage proposal. Nicholas drowned his sorrow in a vodka binge in Dalsia. Sophia orchestrated a wedding, and the drunken heir married her in a simple but legal Russian Orthodox ceremony. The morning after, Nicholas's entourage returned him to Russia to tell his parents. By that time, the czar's health was failing, and he refused to accept this nobody princess's manipulation, especially when Queen Victoria's favorite granddaughter just needed a little convincing to unite two great dynasties. In true Russian fashion, the czar dispatched men to Dalsia to erase the event. Sophia, suspecting something unscrupulous, hid in a convent. The men murdered the priest and a woman who had posed as the princess and returned to Russia reporting success, freeing Nicholas to marry Alix of Hesse."

Did that make Nicholas II a bigamist? "But she didn't die."

"Not in March of 1894. Sophia died in childbirth in October. She delivered twins. A boy and a girl."

"So, Nicholas was free to marry Alix of Hesse in November of 1894."

"Providence worked out for him there. During that original trip, Wilhelm sold Sophia's father a ninety-carat rough for a line of Andalusian horses. This stone became part of Sophia's dowry. Mystics do run in the Dalsian line. Sophia was clearly one in her own right. When she realized Nicholas was not coming back, she split the stone and hid the marriage documents, knowing someday her descendants would take their rightful place. On Sophia's deathbed, her maternal aunt cursed Nicholas and his forthcoming heirs. The prophecy says, 'The bear will fall to peasant rule and rise again in the one-hundredth-and-twentieth year, when the golden suns unite to revive what was once stolen from the soul of the true leader.'"

"That's it? It could mean anything," That I'd been wrong about the diamonds' origins faded in the face of Madame Orr's compelling story.

"Sophia was a strong woman who... The past is the past. Victor wants a reset."

"As if that's possible," I grumbled.

"I know. I have my doubts about Logan, but he is the image of Nicholas II."

No wonder I'd recognized him. "We all know how well that turned out," I had to add.

"Don't remind me. My brother is the kingmaker. You do not question him."

"Why force Logan to marry the current Sophia of Dalsia? You of all people know how arranged marriages work out."

Was it regret I saw flash across Madame Orr's face? "Touché. Poetic justice, I suppose. My husband was chosen for his pedigree. It was not a happy union."

Exactly why arranged marriages had gone out a century ago. "You are asking Logan to do the same."

"The rewards are enormous. It is the price for who we are. I willingly paid it. Only Logan can decide if he is willing too."

A crack in the armor? Maybe Logan had a chance.

"This Sophia of Dalsia is as strong a woman as her great-great-grandmother."

"Is this the psychic speaking?" I asked.

Madame Orr smiled. "I wish I could see the future here."

An interesting comment. "Why not go with Loreli?" If anyone could pull this farce off, she could. "She's the right woman for the job."

"Not in Russia. Victor has been pumping money into the Restore Monarchy Party for years. He has discounted any other heirs for their marrying practices."

"You mean marrying out of their class," I said.

I'd surprised her. "Yes. Then you know a woman can't inherit."

"I do." But I didn't accept it. Hereditary rulers made no sense to me. People proved themselves, period.

"Now you have it, Cat."

The sacrifices of four generations to maintain royalty sat squarely on the shoulders of one man. No wonder Logan felt the pressure. "One last question. What were you looking for in the Barkview City Records room?"

Madame Orr's slow smile drew mine. "You are quite the detective."

I considered that a compliment and thanked her with a nod.

"I wanted to know the legal ownership of the land on the

northeast side of the lagoon," Madame Orr responded.

"The lagoon is city land."

"Not all of it. There's a small parcel on the northeast side that is privately owned. The deed goes back to 1897. It was leased to the City of Barkview for ninety-nine years. It has now reverted back to the legal owners. I wanted to know who the legal owners are."

"Want to buy more property in town?" I asked

"Hardly. Victor tells me a movie is coming to town in the early summer."

"Barkview hosts a lot of movies."

"This one is a 1920s gangster movie about a rumrunner."

"Named Jonathan Douglas?" I groaned. Talk about letting the dogs out. "That'll ensure chaos."

Madame Orr nodded. "It will bring many treasure hunters to town."

"Should help find the Douglas Diamond faster."

"I'd rather not share that story," Madame Orr insisted.

I could understand that.

"Loreli thinks you'll keep their secret," Madam Orr said.

"I will. For an exclusive when Logan comes out," I said.

"I never took you for a glory seeker."

"I'm not. I will tell the story the right way."

"That I have no doubt of." We nodded to each other, an unwritten understanding in place. As we rose to leave, Madame Orr touched my arm. "Discovering your father's fate will change your life. Be sure answers are what you truly seek. The right partner is worth any struggle. He will not be easy, but you can't help who you love."

For a woman with no answers regarding Logan and Loreli, she had a lot to say about my life. Russ took my hand as we walked to his car.

"She can only hurt you if you believe she can," he said.

Did I believe? Maybe a little. More like I wanted to believe I'd someday know the truth about my dad. I took a deep breath. I needed to focus on the goal—finding Chris's killer, and fast. "You don't think she did it, do you?"

"She did not know Chris was a jewel thief," Russ stated.

I had to agree. "The question is, did Adam Smythe or Isaac Samuels know? I'm not buying the coincidence here."

Neither was Russ, based on his head shake. "I'll take another look at Samuels and Sons and check on the file-deleting progress. We need to track Chris's movements the week leading up to his murder."

Ariana had told me that at the start. Why hadn't I listened? "Not so easy with no cameras in town." After this, Aunt Char had to approve some traffic cams. "I don't know where to start."

"Social media," Russ suggested.

The light clicked on. "Sandy." I knew exactly where to find her, too!

Russ nodded. "Meet you at police headquarters in two hours to share notes."

My phone vibrated with a text message alert. From Chelsea Smythe? I quickly read the message. "Chelsea wants me to meet her at Lifeguard Tower One in an hour."

"Why?"

I appreciated Russ's skepticism. Too many unanswered questions pointed toward Adam Smythe's involvement. "Just that she has information I might find useful." I stopped Russ's objection by adding, "Chelsea will talk to me." At least I hoped that's what this olive branch meant. "You keep looking into who deleted the files."

"Take Gem with you." In full agreement with this request, I nodded. Although capable on my own, I felt safer including the guard dog. Odd.

CHAPTER 21

Russ dropped Gem and me at my house, where we found Sandy seated at the counter with her head balanced on her hands, staring at the succulent. What could I say? She'd followed my don't-take-your-eyes-off-it instructions to the letter.

I quickly explained our need to establish Chris's whereabouts last week. Happy to have another task, Sandy dove into the insane world of social media postings to look for what amounted to a needle in a haystack.

I tossed Gem a treat she caught midair and grabbed a Honey Crisp apple from the kitchen counter fruit basket before I took off to speak with Chelsea Smythe, with Gem at my side.

I parked on First Street just south of the Old Barkview Inn and walked along the boardwalk toward the Barkview Cliffs. Usually packed with arm-in-arm strollers, looky-loo tourists, and tandem bicyclists admiring the ocean scenery, the boardwalk was deserted, the gray skies and cool breeze having sent even the hardiest seagulls running for a spot at one of the blazing firepits.

I snuggled deeper into the folds of my oversized sweater as I approached the retro lifeguard shack sitting about a hundred yards off the beach in the soft sand. Originally designed to be a beach changing room around 1920, the pale green and white Victorian shack had been elevated to a lifeguard tower during the surf-crazed 1960s. Nestled closest to the bluffs overlooking the Pacific, tower number one protected the tide pools and coastal cliffs reachable only at low tide.

Gem's ears went wide and then flattened, alerting me to Chelsea's presence even before I noticed her seated on the seawall bench, bundled in a dark wool coat over jeans. A steaming Daily Wag cup in hand, Chelsea gestured for me to sit beside her. "Thank you for coming."

I smelled the café mocha and wished I'd brought my own java, if only to warm my hands. Instead, I buried my fingers in Gem's warm fur. "Your mom loved her afternoon mochas." Not all my memories of Lynda Smythe had been negative.

"Sometimes I think she loved this guilty pleasure more than me." Chelsea raised her cup in salute.

I got it. Melt-in-your-mouth dark Belgian chocolate solved all my life challenges. "Why did you want to see me?"

"For the record, I am not legally required to talk to you."

"Noted." The lawyer in her just couldn't help herself.

"Before I tell you what Ty and I were discussing last night, I'd like to know why my private life suddenly interests you."

Fair question. After the adversarial mayoral campaign, we'd barely exchanged nods in passing. "When a man is murdered and the evidence points to your father..." My bluntness worked. Her gasp sounded like a something-stuck-in-your-throat croak.

"That changes things. Your aunt will thank me for this bit of information."

Chelsea wanted to help Aunt Char? That remained to be seen.

"Contrary to popular opinion, Ty and I weren't arguing." No doubt Chelsea knew my information had to come from Gossip Gabby. "Ty called me yesterday afternoon and told me he had information that would help my dad's congressional run. I agreed to meet him."

"What congressional run?" Adam Smythe, our representative in Congress? I couldn't think about that now.

Chelsea rolled her eyes. "You really are just a reporter looking for answers, aren't you?"

I took her remark as a compliment. "You're only just figuring that out?"

"I guess I am." Had her antagonism softened a tad? Hard to tell in the cold. We both huddled against the wind. "My dad has had his eye on our district's congressional seat for some time. Ty's family is well-connected in Washington politics. His brother is chief of staff for a senator. My mother hired him to help pave the way for when our current congressman retires next November."

That explained Ty's loyalties to Adam Smythe. "Of course, you had to hear him out."

"Of course. Imagine my surprise when he told me the Shepard Diamond was a fake."

I didn't even flinch, much to Chelsea's disappointment. Maybe acting could be a career choice after all. "That's a bomb," I said. "Where did he get that information?"

"I'll let you in on a little secret," Chelsea confided. "Ty always knew far more than anyone should know. I swear half his information came from closed-door meetings that he did not attend. I digress. He claims to have heard your aunt and Angela speaking about it."

Could he have heard the two women speaking through the

heavy mahogany door? With a stethoscope at the lock, maybe. Sandy tended to know more about me than I did sometimes. The tracker in Gem's collar came to mind. Could it be that simple? "That's crazy. You saw the exhibit," I said.

"I did, and the stones were magnificent, but I'm no expert. Isaac Samuels admitted he couldn't even tell the difference without looking at them through a high-magnification loupe or under a microscope."

"Isaac is hardly a diamond expert." Naturally, she'd asked her father's buddy.

"True, but his brother Jacob is."

The brother whose divorce caused the family to lose control of their business. "Did Jacob explain the testing technique?"

"Apparently, the Shepard Diamond has a tiny inclusion under a 30X magnification that would be next to impossible to duplicate."

Only a select number of people knew about that inclusion. "How does Jacob know about it?"

"He claims to have seen the stone's GIA report."

"Doesn't it seem odd that a relatively small-time jeweler had access to a nonpublic report?"

"It does, which is why I called you."

Maybe she was trying to help. The former mayor's influence could make this story front-page news. I could already see the headline: "Small-Town Mayor Covers Up Major Theft."

"Do you intend to request a test?" I asked.

"Please. Fake or not is irrelevant. My father can't afford to be on wrong side of any scandal right now. He was instrumental in getting that diamond brought to Barkview."

Still protecting her dad. I'd do the same for Aunt Char. "This certainly brings Ty's loyalty into question."

"I agree. I don't want any man willing to sell out his

current boss on my staff. I don't know what Dad's been involved with in the past, but loyalty is everything to me."

We agreed on that. "Ty stormed out when you told him that, didn't he?"

"He did. The man's a, well... I see you agree. In my opinion, my father needs to stay clear of him."

A begrudging kinship stirred. We were both trying to protect someone we loved. "Your father's public mayoral files have been, uh, misplaced," I said.

"What?"

She hadn't known. Could Ty, the man who fussed with floral arrangements and seating charts, really be involved? But why, if not at Adam Smythe's request? Could there have been something in Adam Smythe's files that incriminated Ty?

"How do you know?"

"I pulled the public file. It's empty. No date diaries. No appointment reminders. Nothing."

"Could it be digital?"

"Also deleted." I didn't dare tell her when.

Concern replaced her confusion. She surmised the potential misconduct allegations right away.

"Why did your dad initiate bringing the Shepard Diamond to Barkview?"

Chelsea took a deep breath. "Really, Mom did. I told you she believed there was a link between the Shepard Diamond and the missing Douglas Diamond."

"I know your mother's great-aunt was the intended recipient," I added.

My knowledge surprised her. "You are well-informed."

Clearly, not well enough yet. "The Douglas Diamond belongs to the Douglas Foundation when it's found."

"Legally, that depends on where the stone is ultimately found."

"True."

"So, you believe it will be found too."

I did. The same way I knew too many things.

"Mom promised her grandmother she would try to find it," Chelsea explained.

"I still don't understand how bringing the Shepard Diamond to Barkview helps."

Chelsea shrugged. "Me, neither. Dad never questioned Mom. It was easier to just get out of her way when she demanded something."

Spoken from experience. I felt Chelsea's pain. "She was a force of nature."

"She was. I asked Isaac, too. He didn't handle the transaction. His brother Jacob did through their New York office."

"When did this process start?"

"Close to two years ago now."

Interesting timing. Ruby and Jacob had still been married. "How's your dad with a computer?"

"He's a great delegator."

Just like me. Adam Smythe hadn't deleted anything, but he and his FBI brother would know someone who could hack files.

"What about Ty?"

"Nothing special. My parents hired him because of his Washington contacts, not his social media or computer skills. One more thing you should look into." Her voice dropped so low I could barely hear her over the wind. "Ty spent his European holiday after his last congressional staff position at a Geneva rehab facility."

"Drugs or alcohol?" Ty's past didn't really matter so long as it stayed there.

"Yes." She took a long sip of her coffee. "I will deny ever having this conversation."

"My word against yours with no cameras in town."

"Yes. I rather like the quaintness."

So did I, I realized, watching her walk down the boardwalk. Chelsea's information filled in more blanks. I still needed more information, which hopefully Russ could provide. We were getting closer, I could feel it. With any luck I could return the Shepard Diamond soon.

CHAPTER 22

"I think Chris Papas spent last week casing the Old Barkview Inn." Sandy's announcement surprised Russ, Uncle G, and I, as well as the three German Shepherds crammed into the chief's functional precinct office.

Flanked by his two German Shepherds, Uncle G sat behind his smoked-glass desk, his signature toothpick twirling in his mouth as he listened. Autographed photos of two presidents were displayed on the gray wall behind him, a testament to a career well spent. A plasma TV screen overwhelmed another wall.

Gem had herded Sandy and me into straight-backed chairs in the corner and took her position between us and the door. Russ just leaned against the door frame, sniffling. Even an extra dose of Celeste Barklay's allergy pills failed to stop him sneezing from the dander flying everywhere.

I looked up from the trail of pink Post-its I'd laid along the length of the desktop to see Sandy's photo collage on the plasma screen to my right.

"There's a daily post with Chris in the hotel lobby at different times throughout the day," Sandy explained.

"Whom did he meet with?" Uncle G asked.

Sandy shrugged. "Hard to say. The pictures are other guests' vacation photos. Chris is just a bystander."

"Hoping to be found," Russ remarked mid-sneeze. "Notice how he steps into the camera angle in each picture."

I looked closer. Trust Russ for that keen observation. Any wonder I'd come to rely on them? "Franklin, the concierge, should be able to confirm Chris's visits." I jotted a note on a fresh Post-it to ask him and Will personally and stuffed it into my pocket. With any luck, they'd recall who Chris spoke with.

"Did Chris go anyplace else?" Russ asked.

"The Daily Wag on Tuesday and Thursday morning. There's one picture of him walking west on Fourth Street at 12:15 p.m. on Tuesday. Not sure where he's going. He's in a hurry and appears nervous. Look at his expression." Sandy enlarged the picture.

Chris did look like a man on a mission. I shared a knowing look with Russ. Good thing we knew he'd delivered a counterfeit diamond to a demanding client. "Did Chris bring Gem anywhere he went?" It would be interesting to see if the tracker in Gem's collar had actually tracked Chris's movements.

Gem's pointed-ear alertness didn't surprise me. That dog knew when she became the topic of conversation.

Sandy shook her head. Odd. The dog would protect him better than a 9mm handgun.

Russ's critical assessment continued for a moment longer. "Remarkable job, Sandy. If you ever want to get out of TV, call me."

"That will never happen," I confidently replied. Sandy's passion for the news rivaled mine. Russ knew it too.

Sandy's berries-and-cream flush still showed how right on

his compliment was. She'd proven that you couldn't hide, even in a town without cameras.

"Shocking, really, what you can find on social media." I turned to Russ. "Anything on the hacker?"

His exhale didn't instill confidence. "We tracked the IP address through various international locations that ultimately came right back to Barkview. More specifically, the City Hall computer network."

"City Hall?" Russ's confirmation affected my pulse rate. It couldn't be. Sandy and I had been there. Had the old-building-settling noises we'd heard really been another intruder? Gem thought so. I swear her glare said, "I told you so."

Uncle G crossed his arms. "What have you done now?"

I considered ignoring Uncle G's dig, but Russ's pointed gaze demanded I respond. "I, uh, was in the building at the time of the hack."

Uncle G's toothpick snapped. "You?" He couldn't be that surprised. I rarely followed the rules. In my defense, I only broke the rules for a compelling reason. "Never mind. I'm sure you were there on city business." His frown settled on Gem, as if my actions were her fault.

To the dog's credit, Gem stared right back, not giving me away. Sandy inspecting her manicure did.

"Gem wasn't with you?" Uncle G's growl didn't affect my calm, but Russ's tight jaw did. I should've corrected his assumption I had taken Gem with me when I'd had the chance. Now it just looked suspect. I changed the subject. "The only scenario that makes sense is that Chris knowingly stole the fake diamond."

Russ nodded his agreement. "Chris's accomplice must've examined the diamond the moment he brought it up the rope."

"And must have known enough about Chris's past to distrust him. How else would they know to authenticate the diamond? Chris was killed when his accomplice realized the stone was a fake," I said.

"Don't forget the accomplice brought deadly darts on the heist. Unless he planned to kill Chris regardless, since he could identify them." Sandy's suggestion set up my next comment perfectly.

"Then the accomplice had to know about the 30X magnification inclusion. That short list limits our suspects considerably." I discarded a few Post-its and reshuffled them on the desktop. "We have GIA's security chief, Angela Cooper. Madame Orr. Logan and Loreli Roma. Jacob Samuels. Maybe Adam Smythe. I'm sure Chelsea didn't know about it until after Ty told her that the Shepard Diamond was a fake."

"How did he know?" Sandy asked the obvious.

"He claims he heard Aunt Char and Angela talking about it," I replied.

"Not through that heavy door," Sandy said. The absurdity of even thinking that could be true crashed around me.

"Can you do an electronic sweep?" I directed my question to Uncle G but knew Russ would step in. Chelsea's comment about Ty knowing her father's secrets just resonated. I didn't want to believe it. Who bugged rooms in picture-perfect Barkview?

Sandy scrolled through some pictures on her iPad and then reorganized my Post-its yet again. "You need to add Ruby Samuels to the suspect list."

"Why?" I asked "How would Jacob Samuels's ex-wife know about the inclusion?"

"Ruby met Chris at the Old Barkview Inn on Thursday afternoon." Sandy showed a picture of Ruby animatedly gesturing toward a man half-hidden behind a topiary in a lobby alcove. No way to make out the man's face, but his small stature and gray hair looked suspiciously like Chris Papas.

"Samuels and Sons' success is likely the result of Ruby's appraising abilities. The company's losses started at her departure."

Sandy brought the picture of Jacob with his arm around a leggy brunette in question up on the screen beside Jacob. Although the face was obscured, the body shape seemed familiar. "Do you have another picture?"

"I have silhouettes and side views. That's it," Sandy replied.

"Hell hath no fury like a woman scorned," Uncle G said, only half under his breath.

"Ruby still owns twenty percent of the company. It makes no sense to sabotage it," I added.

"Maybe she has another agenda. Since Jacob commissioned the Shepard Diamond copies for Victor Roma, he had a copy of the GIA report." Sandy put up another social media post on the big screen, from two years ago. Jacob Samuels towered over Ruby. "Jacob's left arm was in a sling at the gala. He said he'd been attacked by a dog out running early Friday morning."

"Ariana described one of her assailants as tall and the other short." I'd hardly call Jacob Samuels tall, but next to Ruby... "Why would Ruby or Jacob want the Shepard Diamond? They can't sell it."

"Except to a private collector." Russ scrolled through his phone. "Ruby's past is interesting. She grew up in Colombia. Her parents were missionaries. She worked for an emerald-exporting company, which paid for her GIA degree. She then went to work for De Beers as a diamond grader."

"She never went back to Colombia?" I asked.

Russ shook his head, which got me thinking. No company sent someone to school and didn't require a payback.

"Victor Roma may have wanted the real stone," Uncle G said.

I doubted that. The risks of capture threatened to unravel Victor's master plan.

"The buyer could disguise the Shepard Diamond by recutting it," Sandy suggested.

A tried-and-true way to recreate a treasure. "What would compel Ruby to work with Jacob?" I asked. "At the gala, the word 'civility' barely applied to their interactions. I can't imagine them executing this complicated project together." Not that I blamed Ruby. Trust was everything in a relationship. I glanced at Russ standing tall despite his stuffed-up head and watery eyes, doing his part to solve a murder. Deep down, I knew I could trust him to protect me and mine and always do the right thing. I'd settle for nothing less. The question was, would Ruby settle? What could Jacob have promised to convince her to assist him?

We were missing something in the Chris Papas murder. I could feel it. "How long are Jacob and Ruby staying in Barkview?"

Sandy's computer keyboard clicked. "The GIA Diamond exhibit opens on Tuesday. Samuels and Sons is a listed supporter."

I had two days. Gem's ears flared as I scratched her head. Time for the deceit- detector-dog to meet Jacob Samuels.

CHAPTER 23

Russ insisted on accompanying me to question Jacob Samuels at the Old Barkview Inn. Franklin, dressed in his impeccable Victorian tails, met us at the door. He confirmed Chris's many visits leading up to his murder and said he'd observed him having a discussion with Ruby.

"I apologize, Miss Wright. I did not overhear the conversation. I observed Mrs. Samuels leaving in haste," Franklin admitted.

"You mean she stomped off?" If anyone could stomp in stilettos.

"Yes. She went directly to the bar with Claret, her Russkiy longhair. Magnificent animal," Franklin stated. "Shortly thereafter, Mr. Smythe and Mr. Maynard arrived together."

"Adam Smythe met with Ruby?" My bias aside, Adam just kept coming up. It had to mean something. Didn't it?

Franklin nodded. "I did not hear their conversation, either, but Mr. Smythe left in a hurry. Mr. Ty paid the bill and left shortly thereafter."

"Are Jacob and Ruby getting along?" I asked.

"They appear to be cordial. Mrs. Samuels did request that her room be in a separate wing."

Not the actions of partners. Could they have put aside their differences to work together on the Shepard Diamond heist?

"Is Jacob in his room?" Russ asked.

"I believe he is in the jewelry store with his brother. Mrs. Samuels is out. She has a spa appointment at 2 p.m. this afternoon."

Good to know. Interviewing the brothers together had its advantages. Russ thanked Franklin with a generous tip. We walked through the lobby and down the staircase toward the shopping area. Gem heeled on command, but I felt tension in her every step. We were getting closer. Gem sensed it too.

I paused just before we reached the photo wall. Russ didn't laugh when I explained Gem's initial accusatory reaction to Isaac. "Will you take her? Barkview has no tolerance for aggressive dogs. I'm afraid Gem will attack Chris's murderer."

Russ nodded. "Assuming Jacob is guilty, I doubt even I can hold her back if that is what she has been trained to do."

I bit my lip. He had a point. "She's really a good dog. A bit of a control freak, but she's Ariana's daughter. I can't be responsible for getting her banned from Barkview."

Russ stroked my cheek. "Ariana gave Gem to you to find her husband's killer. She wants answers."

So did I, but not at the cost of Gem's freedom. She was more than a guard dog. She was a member of the family, my family. The realization shocked me. Truthfully, I'd felt the same oneness with my aunt's dog, Renny, and Rayelle's Bichon, too, after our time together, but hadn't recognized the implications until now.

"The bigger problem is evidence. Gem identifying the killer isn't prosecutable," I said.

"I know," Russ admitted. "Knowing where to look will help."

"But it's not a guarantee." No need to bring up the elusive hacker. Russ's team was still working overtime on that lead.

I handed him Gem's leash anyway before continuing to the store. Russ's strength had to be a better choice. We paused at the entrance to the shop. Both brothers stood on the customer's side of the Tahitian pearl counter, speaking in hushed tones.

My fear Gem would pounce on Jacob Samuels didn't happen. Instead, her ears spread out and then lay back flat. Her deep-throated *you're-guilty-of-something* growl sent Jacob and Isaac scrambling for cover behind the glass counter. Not the actions of innocent men.

Of the two, Jacob appeared particularly spooked. He cradled his injured left arm tightly against his body, his wide-eyed stare fixed on Gem's bicuspids. "Get that dog away from me. I'll call security." Real fear sounded in his voice.

I advanced anyway, glad for once that dogs enjoyed privileges in Barkview. "She won't hurt you if you have nothing to hide." I paused well short of the counter. I, of all people, understood the real fear associated with dogs that bite. "I understand you were bitten by a dog."

I swear his Adam's apple bobbed. "Y-yes. I was. I was jogging on the boardwalk at 5:20 Friday morning."

"In the dark?" The fog had been so thick, I could barely see the sand Friday morning. No way had he seen a thing.

"I do not do well with the three-hour time difference between here and New York. I do work with people in Europe daily, you know."

I didn't and didn't care. Arrogance aside, his explanation made sense. The three-hour time lag did make for a rough transition.

"Do you jog every morning?" Russ asked.

"Yes. In Central Park."

So he did have a regular schedule. "Do you always jog when you travel?" I asked.

"Yes. I especially enjoy running on the ocean. I do run by the Loeb Boathouse in the Park."

I glanced at Isaac, arms crossed, dwarfed by his brother, just standing beside him and not saying a word. "Who knew you were jogging Friday morning?"

"No one. I simply woke up and went."

A crime of opportunity or insider planning? Someone who knew him well could have arranged the attack to set him up.

"Dogs don't just jump out of nowhere, bite, and take off." I dropped my elbows on the counter. "What really happened?"

His arrogant lip flare looked suspiciously like a snarl. "I was jogging by the shacks near the lagoon when a white-and-tan mongrel leaped out at me like an apparition."

"A dog ghost bit you?" This story just got better and better. "Did it have a leash or collar on?"

"I did not notice. I never saw the mongrel's owner either. The animal just bit my forearm and disappeared between those wooden shanties."

"Did he bark or growl at you?" Russ asked. "Give you any warning?"

Good point. Someone had to have heard something. Although Stephanie would be annoyed to hear her chic Creamery called a shack, the closely grouped buildings did create tight alleys that could hide a loose dog.

"You expect me to believe a stray dog leaped out of the dark and bit you without provocation, then disappeared the same way it came?" I asked. Verbalized, the story sounded even more implausible.

"It sounds farfetched, but I assure you, it is the truth. I

didn't antagonize the dog. I never saw it coming." He eyed Gem cautiously. "I don't even like dogs."

"Yet you're in business in the dog-friendliest city in America," Russ pointed out.

No wonder the company was failing in Barkview.

"A bad investment." Jacob leveled a glare at his brother who, no doubt, was the guy who'd insisted on opening this branch.

"Why did you open a store in Barkview?" I inquired.

"Lynda Smythe assured me Gem's Palace wasn't meeting the needs of the community." Isaac's nasal tone sounded distinctly whiny.

"What about market research? Gem's Palace is a Barkview icon. It's been in business here for thirty-five years. How could you even think you'd compete?"

"Good questions that our investors want answers to as well." Jacob's icy glare seemed to drop the temperature ten degrees. "I did not kill Chris Papas."

I'm not sure why I believed him. Nothing about Jacob Samuels or his story gave me the warm fuzzies. But, between Gem's almost bored scrutiny and his insane dog bite story, I did. "You knew about the Shepard Diamond's inclusion. You brokered the man-made rough purchase. Why should I believe you?"

"Because it is the truth. Chris Papas proved to be a talented diamond cutter. I'd hoped to use his services in the future," Jacob replied.

No denial. I went for the big question. "Did you know Chris Papas was a jewel thief?"

"A jewel thief?" Only an Oscar-winning actor could appear that shocked.

"Come on, Jacob," Russ said. "You expect me to believe you didn't know? Your company is...having financial difficulties.

Stealing the Shepard Diamond frees you from debt. You have the clientele who can afford to pay your price for the diamond."

Jacob ran his fingers through his coiffured hair. Finally, a break in his armor. "I suggest you speak to Ruby," he said simply.

"Blaming your ex-wife? Not very chivalrous." Russ's words resonated. He'd never throw me under the bus like that.

"What exactly is your relationship with your ex-wife?" I asked.

Jacob paled. "She's trying to destroy us."

Edged with panic, that statement sounded real enough.

"She's a minority partner. How exactly is she doing that?" Russ asked.

"She took the clients she appraised jewelry for to another jeweler. Business is business," Jacob replied.

My annoyance spiked. He didn't know why she was mad? I caught Russ's eye roll. Even Isaac shook his head.

"So your ex-wife, whom you felt had less breeding than her dog, doesn't want to be around you." It was a good thing Russ jumped in. That man needed a good old-fashioned set-down. What an arrogant... Ruby was better off without him.

"Can I also assume that the relationship with the Russian rough supplier belongs to her?" he asked.

"I negotiated the deal." Jacob's sneer said more than his words.

Isaac's dagger glare went right for his brother's jugular. "Ruby knew them from her De Beers days," Isaac added.

"De Beers works with synthetics?" I asked. The biggest diamond consortium in the world worked with fakes? That made no sense.

"No. She had an eye for diamonds."

"She could spot a fake at a glance," Isaac insisted.

"My brother met Ruby at a diamond auction in Tel Aviv. She was something back then. All fire. Ah! Nouveau riche." Jacob turned to his brother. "Tell them about her. You know her best."

Russ and I shared a look over that odd comment. How could a brother-in-law know a woman better than her husband?

"She was a looker. Appraised diamonds like no one you'd ever seen. Never saw an eye like hers." More than brotherly appreciation came through in his manner. Could this have been a love triangle?

"Isaac offered her a job before checking her references. Just another of his many bad decisions," Jacob announced.

Isaac's shoulders hunched. No doubt this was a frequent argument between the brothers.

I couldn't help myself from adding, "You married her."

Jacob sniffed. "Yes. Under false pretenses. Her parents were missionaries."

"She converted to Judaism."

Jacob *harrumphed.*

"Ruby's clients saved you from your bad decisions," Isaac snapped. "Ruby landed some rich clients on the Upper East Side who were afraid to wear their family jewels in public. She facilitated synthetic reproductions."

Jacob's elbow connected with Isaac's stomach. The responding grunt brought Gem to her feet. This sibling rivalry had teeth. Isaac's defense of his sister-in-law screamed that they were more than friends.

"Tell me more about these reproductions," Russ said. "Who cut those stones?"

Watching Russ work always made me realize how much I needed to learn about reading people and facilitating responses. While the Post-its in my pocket always burned to come out, Russ did not write notes. Instead, he filed Isaac's responses in his mental to-be-followed-up-on-later folder.

"We'd never used Chris Papas before," Isaac insisted. "Lynda Smythe suggested Chris Papas cut the Shepard Diamond replica. I don't know why. He turned out to be a good choice. The replica he did was magnificent."

No denying that, nor that a visit with Ruby was in order. I had a good idea who Chris's killers were and why, and so did Russ. That mere identification wasn't going to be enough chafed. Proof beyond a shadow of a doubt required a confession.

CHAPTER 24

I dropped Russ at police headquarters and returned to the Old Barkview Inn. I'd planned to catch Ruby at the spa but aborted that idea the moment I arrived. Gem tore out the car door and sprinted as if pursued by demons, her leash bouncing on the pavement, up the entry steps, and through the lobby. She took a flying leap over a toddler's stroller, undoubtedly freaking out the child's parents, not pausing until she reached the spa. She whined and pawed at the carved Balinese door until I caught up. Franklin had been right about Ruby's appointment. She was there. Don't ask me how I knew, I just did.

My hands on my knees, I sucked in long breaths while attempting to calm Gem. Tension vibrated through the dog's body. She wanted revenge. I got it. I even admired her focus, but right now I needed her cooperation. When my firm talk failed to convince her to back off, I resorted to a stern heel command. It worked. The dog followed me away but frequently looked back over her shoulder.

Who knew I'd ever appreciate good dog training so much? Why had I ever questioned that I would know when Gem found Chris's killers? Whoever said I couldn't adapt to a dog could eat their words today.

Like Russ said, confirming at least one of the culprits helped. Catching the remainder of the conspirators required a neat little setup. I called Russ from my car in the Old Barkview Inn's parking lot. Better I stay parked before having this conversation.

"Ruby's confirmed as a conspirator. I'll call Aunt Char to set up the meeting with Angela. Are you sure no one knows you found the listening device in her office?"

"Yes. The chief and FBI have the building under surveillance. You were right about the synthetic diamond creator being sponsored by the Russian mob. The company is on Homeland Security's watch list."

"Soon to be on the hot list, I hope." The big-pocket connection explained the professional hack job and revived Russ's faith in his own team.

"With Ruby's help, maybe," Russ said. "I'd still be more confident if we had the real stone."

I dreaded it, but the time had come to tell. "About that... Gem, uh, swallowed it." No need to say more, but Russ's silence got to me. Even knowing that technique was meant to make people talk, I still couldn't help myself. "I found it in her poop." Stop talking. He didn't need to know. "Yesterday."

"And you intended to tell me when?"

His disappointment really hurt. "When your responsibilities didn't force you to return the stone before we found Chris's killer. Disagree with me all you want, but I'm right and you know it."

"The end doesn't always justify the means."

It did in this case, and he'd never convince me otherwise. "We can argue about this later."

"I don't argue."

He didn't. He concisely stated his position and invariably made me feel like an idiot. Not this time.

"You took an unnecessary risk. There is a killer looking for the Shepard Diamond."

I should be happy my safety came first. Why did I feel stifled?

"Even now, I don't like the idea of you meeting with Angela alone," Russ said.

"I'm not putting my aunt in harm's way. Besides, Gem will protect me." My hand shook as I stroked the dog's head, trying hard to overlook the fur fallout. This dog would give her life to protect me; a little mess hardly mattered. I had to believe it wouldn't come to that. I just needed to retrieve the real Shepard Diamond from my place and I'd be ready.

I disconnected Russ's call and dialed Aunt Char. "Call Angela." No need to say more. My aunt hadn't liked the plan, but in the end she'd agreed. "Be careful, my dear. Gem, I'm counting on you."

Gem shook her majestic head in total agreement. That I felt better didn't really surprise me.

"I'm in good hands. Remember, I'm just the messenger," I said.

"If there were no risk, I would be the messenger. Don't think I don't know you, Cat Wright."

Never a doubt. I hung up and took the long way home. I needed a few minutes to get my head in the right place to carry out the plan. Aunt Char confirmed that Angela would meet me in fifteen minutes at City Hall as I opened my garage door and drove in. The lack of parking at the beach always made a quick stop at my place a pain. Gem stutter-stepped in the front seat, whining when I ordered her to sit and closed the car door. I had just enough time to grab the succulent and be gone to meet Angela. Gem's ritual house sniff would make me late.

The dog's sudden barking surprised me as I hurried through the garage door into the laundry room. She didn't normally bark without cause. Was she developing separation anxiety? I typed in the alarm code, only realizing mid-entry that no buzzer sounded. My heart pounded. I'd set it. I knew I had. A priceless diamond sat on my counter.

Instinctively, I pivoted to retreat and cracked open the garage door just enough to hear Gem's wild barking when an all-too-familiar voice stopped me cold.

"Come in, Cat. I've been expecting you."

At this moment, being right didn't matter. I forced a smile. "Why, hello, Ty. I'm afraid I can't offer you a Meister Blizzard."

"Jägermeister has always been my downfall. I should've known. Do come inside." The 9mm pointed right at me provided ample encouragement to obey. "Thank you for leaving Gem in the car. Makes this easier."

Colossal mistake on my part. No wonder Gem had wanted to come inside. "Depends on what *this* is."

Me, the gal who falls apart in an emergency, utterly calm? What was happening to me? I was on my own here. I'd left my guard dog in the car in the garage.

"It's a diamond retrieval. Hand it over." Ty's right arm shook as he leveled the gun directly at my heart.

Thanks to Gem's dog bite, I saw a weakness in his grip ripe for exploitation. I also noticed a tornado seemed to have struck my home. Not a single knickknack remained shelved. The chairs had been ripped and sliced. Even my refrigerator and freezer had been emptied onto the counter, barricading the succulent into a corner. Ironic how that had worked out. Hiding something in plain sight did work.

"What makes you think I have the real Shepard Diamond here?" I asked, but I knew. That black tracker I'd found in

Gem's original collar should've tipped me off. Somehow, Ty had planted a listening device in Gem's replacement collar.

"I see you figured it out. I knew you'd replace the collar you destroyed." Ty winced.

"And you made sure I got the last collar in Barkview. How did you get Loreli to buy the other one?"

"I sent her a fashion post. Her Cavalier will be wearing a tutu next week." He flexed his arm. The more the infected dog bite bothered him, the better my chances.

"Why did you kill Chris?" Best to keep him talking. Gem's barking would alert someone eventually.

"I didn't kill Chris." Ty did seem cold as ice.

"So Ruby did." My knowledge either didn't surprise him or he didn't care.

He shifted his weight. "I warned her Chris might swap the stones. When he did, she lost it. Having a temper is never good." He held his left hand up. "Steady as a rock."

Except for the quiver. "You didn't kill Chris. You weren't even there. The worst they can get you on is a breaking-and-entering charge at Gem's Palace and detaining someone against their will. You could plead that to time served."

"You think so?" Ty's superior tone said I'd read that one wrong.

"So you're only in it for the money?"

"A comfortable beach house in the Maldives, to be exact."

"A country with no extradition treaty with the USA."

Ty's smile confirmed it all.

I leaned against the counter and crossed my arms. Bravado alone wasn't getting me out of this one alive. I needed a miracle. If possible, Gem's barking had gotten even more insistent. The periodic thud offered hope. Howard Looc's Border Collie had broken through a car window in his defense. "Not a prayer.

I'm dead the minute you find the diamond." I gestured around the room. "Have at it. Looks like you're not doing so well."

Ty did not break eye contact as he shouted over his shoulder, "Bring Sandy in."

I sucked in my breath. I'd never even considered that she might be a target. My bedroom door opened and Sandy came out, looking pale and oddly annoyed, followed by Ruby pointing a dart gun at the small of Sandy's back. "That Neanderthal shot Jack in my living room." That explained Sandy's anger. Hurting Jack promised retribution.

"With a tranquilizer?" I asked.

"Relax. Ruby won't let me kill a dog," Ty said.

That made some sense. Ruby had a soft spot for dogs. She'd drugged Gem. There was no way she'd hurt Jack. The dog didn't pose a threat. But Ruby did. Too bad her empathy didn't extend to humans. She'd already committed murder; one more wouldn't matter. Sandy's height and age possibly gave her an advantage. So did the location of my couch and coffee table. Just maybe agile Sandy could get away.

My eye strayed to the pathetic succulent. Could I buy some time giving Ty the Shepard Diamond, or would that just expedite our murders? "Do what she says, Sandy. I'll give Ty the diamond. Ruby, I don't blame you for not trusting men. Jacob wasn't honorable. What he did to you was inexcusable." It really was. "And Chris. I can't believe he didn't deliver the diamond."

"He made a deal." Ruby's small voice sounded childlike.

"I'm shocked you trust Ty. He's just like Jacob."

Did her shoulders hunch?

Ty read my plan exactly. Unemotionally, he said, "The diamond or Sandy's life. You decide." Ty aimed his gun in Sandy's direction. Although his hand shook, I couldn't chance a true or lucky shot.

"Okay. Okay." Louder, I said, "Don't be afraid, Sandy. I'll toss him what he wants."

"You'll hand it to me," Ty corrected me. "Very easy."

Not that easy. I'd made my point. Sandy knew to look for a distraction. No choice remaining, I took three steps into the tiled kitchen. My eye wildly took in the frozen bounty on the counters. Could a frozen pork chop take out a 9mm? Did I dare chance it? If I failed, Sandy stood no chance.

I lifted the succulent and picked the Shepard Diamond out of the soil. With exaggerated slowness, I lifted the stone to the light before flicking it airborne, lighting the kitchen in dazzling yellow prisms.

"Dive, Sandy. Dive!" I hit the floor about the same time as the stone tinged against the travertine. It bounced once, twice.

Ruby cursed. Something clunked. A shot fired and footsteps pounded on the floor. OMG! I'd failed Sandy. A heartbeat later Ty rounded the counter, his gun ready.

What they say is true. When you face certain death, your life does flash before your eyes. The good, the bad, and the undone all at once. Russ's smile stayed with me. I felt a single tear roll down my cheek. We deserved a chance at happiness. If I had another chance...

The sound of shattering glass and a to-the-death growl froze time. I don't know exactly what happened, but a black-and-tan blur leveled Ty as a bullet whizzed by my head. Blood splattered everywhere. Had Gem been hit? She'd leaped between me and the bullet. Had she killed Ty? He lay unmoving. If he made a sound, I didn't hear it over the ferocious growling.

"Sandy!" I screamed.

"I'm okay. Ruby, not so much."

Russ and Uncle G flew through the door before I stopped

shaking. Russ plucked me off the floor and crushed me into his embrace. "Are you all right?"

I must've nodded as I clung to him, soaking up his warmth. On Uncle G's command, Gem backed off Ty, her bloody footprints ending where she collapsed, still separating me from Ty.

As the white-uniformed emergency vet techs, a Barkview service I now fully supported, went to work on her, I saw the blood matting the fur on her head. Hers, I imagine, from when she'd broken through the car window to protect me. Maybe Ty's. I wasn't sure. All I knew was that dog had saved my life.

CHAPTER 25

A week later, Sandy and I sat on my oceanfront patio, finally soaking up some afternoon rays and catching up. Jack, still lethargic from the drugs in the tranquilizer dart, lay quietly at her feet.

"Let me see it again." Sandy grabbed my left hand and held it up to the light. "I can't believe you said yes."

Neither could I. No self-respecting blingaholic could turn down the four-carat sparkler Russ put on my hand, even if it was a Barklay hand-me-down. The engagement ring worn by generations of Barklay brides now belonged to me. Aunt Char had insisted when Russ requested her permission to marry me. Wish I'd overheard that planning session. Russ dropping to a knee at Aphrodite's Haven on Ariana's porch touched me too.

"Must've been a weak moment." I still couldn't quit smiling. In the end, I think I demanded he marry me.

Sandy giggled. "You didn't have a chance. You owed Gem, and she insisted."

"I think she just wanted someone else to be my keeper." The German Shepherd's bandaged head had nudged my hand into Russ's, not budging until he slipped the ring on my finger. She then limped, favoring her injured paw, to Ariana's side and sat with finality as if to say, "Well done!" That Ariana just stood there beaming made me wonder if she'd planned it from the start.

I still couldn't be mad. Ariana had chosen to leave witness protection and stay in Barkview. With Chris gone, someone seeking revenge seemed unlikely. Besides, why start over when she'd found her family. She'd even made great progress remodeling the jewelry store and planned to reopen next month.

A grateful Angela upped Aunt Char's political equity by arranging for her to cut the ribbon opening the GIA's international colored-diamond exhibit, featuring the Shepard Diamond. The Samuels brothers' absence went unnoted. In fact, Firebird Industries pulled the jewelry store's funding, essentially bankrupting them. No doubt thanks to Madame Orr.

"Did you see that photo of Loreli's Cavalier in a silver tutu? It got something like a million hits," Sandy said.

I swallowed a chuckle. "Yeah." I'd been one of the many. "Ty missed his calling."

"Where he's going, he'll have lots of time to think up new fashion statements."

"He'll be an old man before he gets out, between charges of aggravated murder, unlawful restraint, and disrupting public service for causing the water main break," I agreed, relieved. "I still can't believe he orchestrated the file deleting."

Sandy shook her head. "The feds will be looking into that scheme for sure. Logan's engagement to Princess Sophia of Dalsia sure got the pickleball sites talking too. Do you think he'll retire?"

I nodded, disappointed but not surprised. What could I say? He'd made his choice. "I'm stunned the former mayor escaped without a mark on his reputation." That Chelsea had even congratulated me on my engagement and given me her mother's diaries about the Douglas Diamond shocked me even more. Much as I wanted to know about Lynda's involvement with the Shepard Diamond, I also knew it didn't matter. The woman was deceased.

"If Madame Orr is right and the Douglas Diamond will be found this year, we'd better get serious," Sandy said.

I handed her the leather-bound diaries. "I didn't see anything new."

"Do you still think the secret beach where Jonathan proposed to Marie is the key?"

"I have a feeling." I hated to admit it. After my near-death experience, I wasn't ready for another hair-graying adventure just yet. This journey I seemed to be on needed a tame next step. Sure, I'd enjoyed parts of each experience. In the end, the couch potato Cavalier slowed down my lifestyle. The high-maintenance Bichon Frise had been a tad too much. Seriously, I couldn't spend more time grooming my dog than myself. With Russ around, an overprotective German Shepherd would put me over the edge. Maybe, deep down, I'd always be a cat person. If so, I'd already used two of my nine lives.

"Say no more. I'll pull every topographical map for a fifty-mile radius. We'll find that beach."

I had to love Sandy's enthusiasm. I could count on her to run with the plan. When she found something, I'd be ready to rejoin the hunt for the Douglas Diamond. It wasn't going to be easy, but we were going to find it. I knew it.

"What beach are you looking for?" An all-too-familiar voice drew my eye to the boardwalk patio entry. A cavernous suitcase on wheels at her side, a tawny-haired woman with hazel eyes peeking over reflective Maui Jim sunglasses smiled at me. "Maid of honor reporting for duty, Sis."

Furballs! This couldn't be good.

The End 🐾🐾🐾

Join Cat on her quest for the perfect dog when she teams up with a Golden Doodle to solve a hundred year old mystery and find the long lost Douglas Diamond in ***Doodled to Death***.

Hope you enjoyed your adventure in the dog-friendliest place in America. To learn more about Barkview and Cat's next adventure visit: www.cbwilsonauthor.com.

Sign up for ***The Bark View*** a monthly update all things Barkview including:

- *Friday Funnies*, pet related cartoons
- Recipes from *Bichon Bisquets Barkery's* canine kitchen
- Cool merchandise ideas from the *Bow Wow Boutique*.
- Not to mention Barkview news and fun contests.

Don't miss Cat's next adventure:

COMING SOON: DOODLED TO DEATH

A BARKVIEW MYSTERY

A lost diamond, a century old betrayal and a murdered treasure hunter can't possibly derail a Barkview female aviator's induction into the National Aviation Hall of Fame. But, the recent evidence paints Sky Barklay as a murderer. A hundred years after the fact, who would frame her?

Cat Wright has her own family issues. When her sister is accused of murder, Cat discovers that someone doesn't want the elusive Douglas Diamond found. Armed with Sky's diary, Cat learns that the roaring twenties weren't as prosperous or carefree as advertised. In fact, Barkview's five founding families have some skeletons. Question is just how far will someone go today to keep those secrets.

Can Cat and her Golden Doodle partner go back in time, find Jonathan Douglas's murderer and clear Sky before the real killer buries the evidence forever?

ACKNOWLEDGMENTS

To my writing cheerleaders, who endlessly listened to my ideas, edit my spelling and grammar, help research and recipe test, thank you Pam Wright, Dee Kaler, and Brandi Wilson.

For research and police procedure assistance, thank you Richard R. Zitzke, Chief of Police, Whitehall, Ohio, retired. I assure you any errors are entirely my fault. Thank you to all my excellent instructors at the GIA. Diamonds are amazing.

ABOUT THE AUTHOR

C.B. Wilson's love of writing began after she read her first Nancy Drew book and reworked the ending. Studying at the Gemology Institute of America, she discovered a passion for researching lost, stolen and missing diamonds. The big kind. Her fascination with dogs and their passionate owners inspired Barkview, California, the dog-friendliest city in America.

C.B. lives in Peoria, AZ with her husband. She is an avid pickleball player who enjoys traveling to play tournaments. She admits to chocoholic tendencies and laughing out loud at dog comics.

Connect with C.B. Wilson:

www.cbwilsonauthor.com

www.barkviewmysteries.com

Facebook: www.facebook.com/cbwilsonauthor

AUTHORS NOTE

Have you ever ask yourself "what if"? From the first moment I saw the Shepard Diamond at the Smithsonian, the diamond's unknown origin intrigued me. Creating a past for the stone came naturally.

The Smithsonian and GIA procedures for transferring diamonds have been manipulated to fit the story. Diamonds are graded as flawless if it has **no inclusions or blemishes visible under 10x**. An inclusion seen in the Shepard Diamond at 30X is in my imagination.

Laboratory-grown diamonds are real and are not fake diamonds. They are made from 100% carbon and have the exact same chemical properties as mined diamonds. The differences between Natural and Lab Grown Diamonds cannot be seen with the naked eye. Only Natural Diamonds have tiny amounts of nitrogen which is one of the signifiers gemologists use to identify if a diamond is lab grown or natural. In other words, the real diamonds are not perfect!

The German Southwest African mines did export

diamonds to Europe from 1880-1918. There is no official record of a ninety carat yellow diamond existing from the area.

Russian history leading up to the revolution also fell into place. Nicholas II of Russia and Alix of Hesse did marry on Nov 26, 1894. Alix did refuse his marriage proposal several times starting in 1890. She rejected his suit again in April 1894, but changed her mind when Kaiser Wilhelm intervened. Alix officially accepted Nicholas's proposal on April 20, 1894.

Nicholas II was reportedly a faithful husband, but did on occasion over indulge in vodka. He was an avid horseman who preferred Akhal-Teke horses. A trip to recover from Alix's refusal to marry him and purchase horses is not historically accurate.

Russian hereditary is based on dynastic succession. Which means only members of the Russian Imperial House of Romanov can claim rights to the throne and must be first of all born in an equal marriage – between descendants of royal dynasties.

The Monarchist Party of Russia does exist. A study conducted by the All-Russian Center for Public Opinion showed that almost one third of the Russian population favor a restoration as of 2013.

The kingdom of Dalsia does not exist.

Pickleball really was reportedly named after a dog. Maybe... there is some controversy there, too.

BOOKS BY C.B. WILSON

Jack Russelled to Death

Cavaliered to Death

Bichoned to Death

Shepherded to Death

Doodled to Death

Corgied to Death (Coming 2023)